Taking Sides

D0494523

BRIAN GALLAGHER is a full-time writer whose plays and short stories have been produced in Ireland, Britain and Canada. He has written extensively for radio and television and for many years was one of the scriptwriters on RTÉ's *Fair City*.

He collaborated with composer Shaun Purcell on the musical, *Larkin*, for which he wrote the book and lyrics, and on *Winds of Change* for RTÉ's Lyric FM.

His first book of historical fiction for young readers was *Across the Divide*, set in the Dublin Lockout, 1913.

He lives with his family in Dublin.

A Boy. A Girl.
A Nation Torn Apart.

Taking Sides

Brian Gallagher

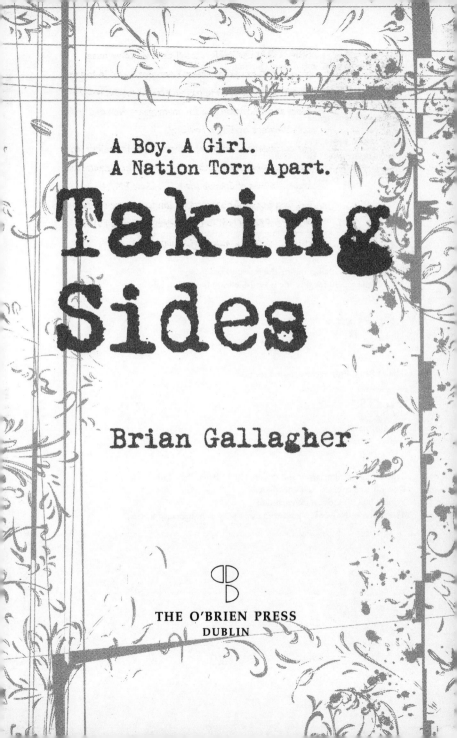

THE O'BRIEN PRESS
DUBLIN

First published 2011 by The O'Brien Press Ltd,
12 Terenure Road East, Rathgar, Dublin 6,
Ireland.
Tel: +353 1 4923333; Fax: +353 1 4922777
E-mail: books@obrien.ie
Website: www.obrien.ie

ISBN: 978-1-84717-279-2

British Library Cataloguing-in-Publication Data
A catalogue record for this title is available from the British Library

1 2 3 4 5 6 7 8
11 12 13 14 15

The O'Brien Press receives assistance from

Typesetting, editing, layout and design: The O'Brien Press Ltd
Cover image courtesy of iStockphoto
Printed by CPI Cox and Wyman Ltd
The paper in this book is produced using pulp from managed forests.

Dedication

To Pat and Hugh.
Thanks for all the years of friendship.

Acknowledgements

My sincere thanks to Michael O'Brien for his proposal of a children's
historical novel set during Ireland's Civil War, to my editor, Mary Webb,
for her insightful suggestions, and to all the staff at The O'Brien Press
who made working on this book a pleasure.
I'm greatly indebted once again to Annie-Rose O'Mahony and
Sean Pardy, two young readers who generously took the time to go
through the first draft and record their observations for me.
My thanks also go to the late Ethna Barror for sharing her memories of
nineteen twenties Dublin, and to Hugh McCusker for his painstaking
proof-reading.
And, as ever, my deepest thanks go to my family,
Miriam, Orla and Peter, for all their support.

PROLOGUE: MAY 1921

— — — — —

NORTH EARL STREET, DUBLIN.

Peter was nervous as he queued at the checkpoint. As a thirteen year-old schoolboy he was unlikely to be roughed up by the soldiers who had suddenly cordoned off the street, but the Black and Tans who manned roadblocks and checkpoints were notoriously lawless and unpredictable, and he felt his heart starting to beat faster.

The War of Independence had been raging for two and a half years between the British Government and the Irish Republican Army, and the Tans were mercenary troops who had been drafted into Ireland to boost the British Army. Peter and his school friends had heard whispered, hair-raising stories about the Tans' treatment of prisoners, and drunken Tans had been known to kill people who had simply annoyed them.

Peter looked towards the head of the checkpoint now and tried to weigh things up. It was mid-afternoon, so the chances were that the Tans wouldn't be drunk this early. The other good thing was that they were under the command of a regular British officer. Peter knew that the British Army behaved far more properly than units like the Black and Tans, who had been recruited – so rumour had it – from jails all over England.

But even the regular army could behave badly, and feelings were running high right now. Two days previously the British had ambushed a rebel unit in Mayo, shooting dead six volunteers, and Peter had just heard a newsboy calling out the latest headline – that in retaliation a party of Royal Marines had been killed today in County Clare.

Was that why the man directly ahead of Peter in the queue was so nervous? There were lots of rebel gunmen walking the streets of Dublin. Could this man be one of them? He was in his twenties and reasonably well dressed, but he was heavily built and looked quite tough – just how Peter imagined a gunman should look. More tellingly, Peter had seen a fleeting look of fear on the man's face when the soldiers had set up the checkpoint. The man had immediately glanced behind him as though to change direction, but the Tans had cordoned off the street to the rear, to prevent any such action.

Peter watched the man carefully. Although he was moving in line with everyone else towards the checkpoint, Peter could see his eyes darting about, still seeking an escape route. From the junction with Marlborough Street to Nelson's Pillar, all of North Earl Street was lined with shops, but if the man hoped to take shelter in one of them he was too late. Peter watched as a line of soldiers fanned out along both sides of the street, to ensure that nobody left the checkpoint queue to enter a shop.

The man looked ahead again, as though gauging how long he

had before reaching the checkpoint, where people were being frisked and having their bags searched. It was a mild day, but the man wore a heavy jacket, and Peter saw him unbutton it now. Was he too warm, or could he be hoping to get rid of a weapon? Peter looked more closely at him. Tiny beads of sweat had formed on his forehead and his jaws seemed to be clenched tightly. But the thing that made Peter's pulses race was the way he had slipped his hand inside his jacket. Surely, even if he had a gun, he couldn't hope to shoot his way past all of the armed soldiers at the checkpoint? He'd be dead before he got a few yards, Peter reckoned, and innocent civilians could get shot too.

The queue moved nearer the waiting Tans, and suddenly Peter felt a movement at his kitbag. At the same time, the man turned round towards Peter, staring him straight in the eye. It was an aggressive, threatening look, and Peter swallowed hard.

'Don't look down,' said the man. He spoke quietly, but with menace.

Peter felt further movement at his kit bag, and realised that the man was slipping something – presumably his weapon – into it. All the while the man stared Peter in the eye, as though daring him to object. Peter felt intimidated, and before he could decide what to do, he felt another movement as the top of his kitbag was closed.

The man spoke again.

'Don't make a fuss, son. Don't even think about it. Right?'

Peter felt mesmerised by the man's frightening stare and somehow he couldn't make himself look away.

'Right?' repeated the man.

'Y ... yes ...'

'You'll sail through; they won't bother a young lad.'

Peter felt really scared, but he didn't know what this man might do if he disobeyed him. He wished that he had never gone near North Earl Street. He had been coming home from an away rugby match with his school, Belvedere, and had stopped off to buy sweets before getting the tram home to Glasnevin. Now, though, he had landed himself in real trouble. He thought of what the man had said about the soldiers not bothering a young lad. But the previous November, eighteen-year-old rebel Kevin Barry – a former pupil at Peter's school – had been hanged for his part in the War of Independence.

Before he could think any more about it, the queue moved forward. He moved with it, conscious that he was taking a major risk, but not knowing what else to do. Although there was a lot going on to distract people, it was still possible that someone in the queue could have spotted that he had accepted the weapon. Supposing that person turned them in to the Tans? It didn't bear thinking about. But most Dubliners hated the Black and Tans and their brutal behaviour, and Peter tried to convince himself that even if they had been seen, nobody would say anything.

The queue moved forward again, and now Peter felt beads of sweat on his own forehead. He wiped them with his sleeve; it would be important to appear relaxed when dealing with the soldiers. The queue continued to snake forward, and Peter could hear the harsh tones of the Tans as they questioned and searched people. Those in the queue were being dealt with at a reasonable speed, however, and Peter realised that the soldiers were questioning and frisking all the men, but examining the bags of only about half of the women. *He would have to behave as though there was clearly no need to search the kitbag of a schoolboy.* But even as he thought it, he could feel his heart pounding.

Suddenly, the gunman reached the head of the queue and the soldiers began to question him. Peter noticed that the man kept his replies neutral, not seeking to please, as some people did, but not deliberately provoking the Tans with sharp answers either. Peter was so preoccupied that he didn't reply at first when a nearby voice asked, 'Victory or defeat?'

The voice was cultured, and the accent English, and Peter realised that he had been addressed by the British officer in command. Presumably the man had returned to the checkpoint after deploying the troops who were preventing people from leaving the queue. Peter turned to face his questioner. The Englishman was younger than Peter had first thought, and the officer had kindly blue eyes and a slightly wispy moustache.

'Sorry?' said Peter.

'Belvedere Rugby Club,' said the man, indicating the kitbag. 'Win your match?'

'Yes, 12-9,' answered Peter, and he smiled, despite his nervousness.

'Good show,' said the officer. 'Let me guess,' he added, looking at Peter appraisingly. 'Playing at centre?'

'Yes, actually.'

It wasn't entirely true – he played the occasional game as centre but more often played as out-half, but Peter sensed that this wasn't the time for corrections.

'Score today?'

'No. But I stopped a certain try for them.'

The officer smiled again. 'That's the stuff.'

The man seemed so genuinely pleasant that Peter found it hard to think of him as the enemy. *But that would all change if they opened the kitbag.*

Just then, Peter saw the gunman being dismissed by the soldier who had been questioning him. Now he was next in line. He found himself facing a tall Black and Tan who wore a sergeant's stripes and who stared coldly at him. The man had a scar running from his left eye to his cheekbone, and Peter felt his stomach tighten with anxiety as the man beckoned him forward.

'Coming from?' asked the soldier, in what Peter recognised as a north of England accent.

'St Michael's college.'

'Where's that?' queried the Tan impatiently.

'Ballsbridge.'

'Going to?'

'Glasnevin. My home – Botanic Lodge,' Peter added nervously, in case Glasnevin might not be detailed enough for the scary-looking soldier.

'Arms out,' ordered the man.

Peter lowered his kitbag and stepped forward to be frisked, his mind racing with the thought that if the sullen Black and Tan was thorough enough to frisk a schoolboy, he might well insist on searching the kitbag.

'It's all right, sergeant. I think he's been man-handled enough for one day on the rugger pitch,' said the officer with a smile.

'Very good, sir,' answered the Tan with a hint of disapproval.

Peter smiled back at the young Englishman. He was hugely relieved that the officer was taking his part, but he realised that he mustn't appear *too* relieved, and that he ought to keep things casual-sounding.

'Thanks. I got enough tackles from their flanker.'

'I'll bet.'

'Just the kitbag then,' said the sergeant, indicating the table on which people had been placing their bags for examination.

Peter felt his stomach tighten. Any sort of a decent search would locate the weapon — and he couldn't count on the scar-faced sergeant shying away from rummaging through his soiled rugby gear. Peter hesitated. If he appealed to the officer it might look like he had something to hide. But if he said nothing, hoping for the officer to intervene again, and the man didn't, what then?

'Let's be having you,' said the Tan, his impatience obvious.

Peter had no choice but to hoist the bag onto the table. He wished fervently that he'd never found himself behind the gunman, wished that he hadn't bothered with buying sweets and instead had gone straight home to the safety of his family.

'Open it,' instructed the soldier.

Peter decided to look appealingly at the officer. He caught the eye of the young Englishman, who held his gaze. It only lasted a second or two, but it seemed an eternity to Peter, as he waited for some kind of response. The officer finally raised an eyebrow in a sort of ironic gesture, as if to say *What can you do with someone like the sergeant?*, then he turned to the other man.

'I think you can spare yourself the muddy rugby gear, sergeant,' he said.

'If you say so, sir,' answered the man, his disapproval more obvious this time.

'I do.'

'Yes, sir,' said the man, more respectfully, then he pushed the bag back to Peter.

Don't show how relieved you are! Peter told himself, even though his whole body was flooded with relief.

'Thank you,' he said politely, but casually, to the officer.

'You're welcome. Keep giving the flankers the slip.'

'I'll try,' said Peter, with a smile. Then he picked up his kitbag, nodded to the young Englishman and walked off.

At the corner of Marlborough Street he saw the gunman pretending to be window-shopping. As Peter approached, the man indicated with a nod of his head to turn the corner. Peter followed him, turning left again as the man led the way towards a small laneway that smelt of rotten fruit. Now that the first surge of relief had subsided a little, Peter was more aware of the risk he had taken. But even though it was terrifying to think of what could have happened, it was exciting too, now that he had gotten away with it. *Wait till he told his friends, Tommy and Susie, they would hardly believe him!* Though of course he would have to swear them to secrecy – his parents would go mad if they knew what he had just done.

His thoughts were interrupted by the gunman, who had stepped into the shelter of a doorway that Peter reckoned must be a rear entry to one of the shops on North Earl Street.

'Get in out of view,' said the man, and Peter stepped into the doorway and out of sight of those passing by on Marlborough Street.

'Let's have it,' said the man, indicating the kitbag.

'Right …,' said Peter, then he opened the bag and handed a wrapped parcel to the man. Peter was certain that it was a pistol, but the gunman quickly pocketed it. Before Peter could ask any questions, the man looked him in the eye.

'What's your name?'

'Peter Scanlon.'

'You did well, Peter.'

'Thanks.'

'But what just happened, never happened, if you know what's good for you. Got me?'

'Eh … yeah.'

'Forget me, forget my face, forget any of this ever took place. All right?'

'Right.'

'Good lad. Up the Republic.'

The gunman gave Peter a farewell nod, then turned away and strode briskly up the lane.

Peter stayed unmoving in the doorway. *Forget any of this had happened?* Not in a million years. It had been terrifying, no question, and he still felt a little shaky. But it was thrilling to realise that he had outsmarted the dreaded Black and Tans, and to know that he had played a part, however small, in the War of Independence. Excited by the thought, he stepped out of the doorway, swung his kitbag over his shoulder and started on the journey home.

PART ONE

A CHANGE IN THE AIR.

CHAPTER ONE

━ ━ ━

MAY 1922
ST MARY'S NATIONAL SCHOOL,
DUBLIN.

'Annie Reilly! Stand up.'

Annie rose from her desk and faced the teacher, Miss Moynihan, who stood at the blackboard.

'Are you day-dreaming or doing geography?'

'Doing geography, Miss,' answered Annie, hoping that she could bluff it out, even though she *had* been daydreaming.

'Really? What did I say was the capital of Denmark?'

Annie spirits rose a little. 'Copenhagen, Miss,' she replied, feeling at least ninety per cent confident that this was the right answer.

'Correct city,' said Miss Moynihan. 'Except that I hadn't been talking about Denmark at all. So you *were* daydreaming.'

What if I was? Annie felt like saying. Did the teacher really expect her to concentrate on geography, today of all days? Surely she must know what was at stake, with the scholarship results due to be announced?

While Miss Moynihan had droned on at the blackboard, Annie had been thinking of how her life would change if she won a scholarship. At twelve years of age she was the youngest in a family of seven children, and all of the others had left school by the time they were fourteen. Though this wasn't just the norm in Annie's family – none of the other boys and girls on her road had gone to a fee-paying secondary school. And even if she won the scholarship that would pay for her to attend Eccles Street convent, it would still be a stretch for her family to find money for extras like books, sports gear and a new uniform. Even so, she knew it would be a dream come true for Ma and Da to see her going on to the highly regarded convent school.

'I expect you to set an example, Annie,' said Miss Moynihan.

If the good pupils don't, who will? Annie said to herself, in what was the teacher's usual mantra.

'If the good pupils don't do so, who will?' continued the teacher predictably.

'Sorry, Miss,' answered Annie politely, even though she was annoyed with Moynihan. She reckoned that the lanky teacher – Beanpole was her nickname – must be at least fifty, so you'd think by now she would know how unfair it was to Annie, or any other pupil, to be singled out as a shining example to all the other girls. Even though Annie was fairly popular most of the time, she could sense the resentment of her classmates when Miss Moynihan made her out to be better than them.

It was the same with her friends on the street. When she told them she was trying to win a scholarship, one boy had asked her if she thought the local school wasn't good enough for her. Annie had tried to explain that it wasn't like that, but that the scholarship was a prize she would be mad not to claim if she could. She had tried to make them understand, but she knew that they felt she was considering herself as different, and that even her old friends mightn't be all that eager for her to succeed.

'Very well, Annie,' said Miss Moynihan, 'you may sit down. So … the principal cities of the Netherlands. Cissy Fanning, what's the main Dutch port?'

'Rotterdam, Miss.'

Cissy was the other pupil that the teacher regularly held up to the class and, sitting down again at her desk, Annie was relieved to have the focus taken off herself.

'Well done, Cissy,' said Miss Moynihan. 'Now, the biggest Dutch city is Amsterdam, but it's not the capital. Can anyone else tell me what it is?'

It was on the tip of Annie's tongue to say 'The Hague' but she deliberately kept quiet. She watched the look of annoyance on the teacher's face when one of the slower girls in the class cried out 'Hamburg, Miss?' Before Beanpole could point out sarcastically that Hamburg was in another country – as Annie knew she would – there was a knock on the classroom door, and Mr Creedon, the Principal, walked in.

Mr Creedon was a stout man with old-fashioned whiskers and a country accent that was still as strong as the day he left his native County Kerry many years ago. He seemed to believe that the children thought he had a good sense of humour, but Annie felt he was really silly, and so did most of her classmates. Still, they were glad of the diversion whenever he came into the classroom, and so they always laughed at his jokes, however feeble.

'Sorry to interrupt, Miss Moynihan,' he said now with the kind of exaggerated politeness that the teachers used when talking to each other in front of the pupils. 'And sorry, class, for interrupting ye,' he continued, turning smilingly to the children. 'I know ye hate anything that halts the lessons, don't ye?'

The children laughed dutifully, but Annie couldn't join in, knowing that the principal had probably come to announce the scholarship results.

'Well, don't ye?' he persisted.

'Yes, Mr Creedon,' they called out in unison.

'I won't keep ye from the …' he paused and looked at the writing on the blackboard to see what they had been studying. 'I won't keep ye from the geography any longer than I have to. I know ye wouldn't want that,' he said, trying for and getting another laugh. 'Well, I have a piece of good news. The scholarship results have just been announced.'

Annie felt her pulses racing. Obviously a scholarship had been awarded, but was it to her or to Cissy Fanning?

'Sixth class in St Mary's has a very bright young lady in its midst. She's brought honour to the school, to Miss Moynihan here, and to herself and her family. And I know she'll use the scholarship to further her studies to the very best of her ability.'

Annie felt that her thumping heart must be audible to the girl sitting beside her, but she tried to show no emotion. If Cissy was the winner she would have to congratulate her, and not let her own bitter disappointment show. And if she won she would have to try to be modest, and not make Cissy feel bad by seeming to gloat.

'Being granted a scholarship is a great opportunity, not given to many. But I know this year's winner will grasp the chance to make her dreams come true.'

Annie felt her chest tighten with tension as the principal's words hit home. Because she *had* a dream. Even though she had never told another soul, in her dreams she imagined going on to college and becoming a teacher. None of her friends, none of her family, no-one she knew had gone to college, and Annie had kept her dream to herself for fear of ridicule. And now her whole future was going to be decided by what Mr Creedon announced.

'Well, I think I've kept ye all in the dark long enough,' he said with a smile. 'Time to announce the name. This year's scholarship winner is … Miss Annie Reilly!'

* * *

Peter had a secret that he couldn't share with his father. His brothers Francis and John had followed the family tradition of dentistry, and Peter knew that he was expected to do the same – but he just couldn't. Neither of Peter's sisters had done so, but that hadn't been a problem. His eldest sister, Anne, was married to a solicitor, and before getting married she had been a school teacher, as was his other sister, Maura, who taught in the nearby Holy Faith convent in Glasnevin. There was a strong tradition, however, of male Scanlons being dentists, and Peter was conscious that he would be the first of his generation to break it. It was simple, really – he was squeamish when it came to blood and drills and other implements that probed into people's gums. He had even become slightly weak when they had dissected a frog in biology class in school. He hadn't admitted it to his friend Tommy or any of the other boys in his class, and certainly not to his father. It didn't make sense to Peter, who was an unflinching rugby player and had no fears about injuries or blood on the playing field. For some reason, though, cutting open people's gums and drilling into their teeth made him feel really queasy.

Today being a Wednesday, it was his dad's half-day from the surgery, and he would soon be heading off for his regular game of golf. Now, though, his father was talking about college, and Peter felt uncomfortable. He sat with his parents at the kitchen table as the May sunshine flooded the room, the summer light dappled by the tall trees that acted as a boundary between the family's long back lawn and the adjoining grounds of the Botanic Gardens. The fact that their nice house and good lifestyle was all funded by his father's dental practice wasn't lost on Peter, but he knew that dentistry as a career wasn't for him. He wasn't sure what he *did* want to do, which made it that bit harder to resist his family mapping out his future.

'So, what's the plan this afternoon, Peter?' asked his father.

'We've a match at half-three.'

'I meant your study plans. You've still Latin and English in your summer exams, haven't you?'

'Yes,' answered Peter, 'but I'll study before I go, and then some more when I get back.'

'Make sure you do. Don't want to fall at the last fence, eh?'

'No, Dad.'

'Good man.'

'Actually, I might go up and make a start. Can I be excused, Mum?'

'*May* I be excused, Peter,' corrected his mother, her tone mildly admonishing.

'May I be excused?'

'Yes, but don't cut it too fine for getting to the sports grounds.'

'I won't,' said Peter, then he rose from the table, wished his father good luck with the golf, and left the room. He took the stairs two at a time, entered his bedroom and closed the door behind him. He would have a quick look at his Latin before he left for rugby, but right now he wasn't in the mood for verbs and grammar. Instead he reached under his bed and retrieved one of his scrapbooks. He took last night's newspaper from his desk at the window and then picked up the large scissors that lay beside it.

Ever since the incident with the Black and Tans a year previously, he had cut photographs and articles out of the newspapers for his scrapbooks, and his parents had been happy to indulge it as a harmless hobby that reflected an interest in history. They would have been shocked if they realised that his interest wasn't just in recording events, but that his appetite had been whetted to play a part in them too.

He looked at the headline of the piece that he was cutting out and read it again. *Collins Tries To Prevent Civil War*. He had once hero-worshipped Michael Collins, who had led the guerrilla fighters in the War of Independence. But now Collins had negotiated a treaty with Britain to found an Irish Free State. *How could he?* thought Peter. How could he accept deputies in the new parliament still swearing allegiance to the King? And the six counties of Northern Ireland still being in the United Kingdom? It was no wonder a civil war was looming.

Already, pro- and anti-Treaty forces had killed each other, with both sides trying to take over barracks and weapons being left by the departing British. But although Peter hated the idea of former comrades now being enemies, he had no doubt about which side was right. The men who had taken on the Black and Tans and were ready to fight again for full independence were his heroes now. And if it *did* come to war, this time he didn't want to watch from the sidelines. He wasn't sure how he could play a part, and he would definitely have to keep it from his pro-treaty family, but somehow he *would* find a way.

He took up the article and pasted it into his scrapbook, his mind buzzing with possibilities.

✳ ✳ ✳

Annie walked excitedly towards Drumcondra Road. Back at the school she had felt sorry for Cissy Fanning and had tried to be nice to her, but the news about her own scholarship was still brilliant. Soon she would share it with Ma and Da, and in one way she could hardly wait. But another part of her liked savouring it alone, and she was enjoying the walk home and the anticipation of breaking her good news.

It was hard to believe that she would soon be finished in St Mary's. She had spent the last eight years at school there, and could still remember vividly her first day as a Junior Infant, and Ma smilingly waving her off when she left her in the care of her first teacher, Miss Delaney. All that would be ending now, and while Annie looked forward to going to Eccles Street, she was nervous too, knowing she would be starting from scratch with new girls, some of whose families would be far wealthier than her own.

Up to now, she hadn't given much thought to being either poor or wealthy. She had been the same as all the other children who lived in the narrow terrace of modest houses that was St Alphonsus Avenue, or in the cottages around the corner, that ran down St Josephine's Avenue to the railway bridge. She knew, of course, that posh people lived in fancy houses not too far away in Glasnevin, and that even a couple of streets away from her own door, well-off families lived comfortably in spacious homes. But then, just a little nearer to the city centre, lots of other families lived in horrible tenements, so Annie had felt that her family, the Reillys, wasn't doing too badly.

She crossed the broad thoroughfare of Drumcondra Road, avoiding where the cobblestones were fouled with strong-smelling dung from the horse-drawn milk floats and bakers' carts that plied in and out of town. She waited in the middle of the road until the city-bound tram clanked past, then she made her way past the entrance to Drumcondra railway station before turning left into the narrow confines of St Alphonsus Avenue. She loved how it was like stepping into another world once you entered the avenue and left behind the noise and the bustle of the busy main road. She greeted Josie Gogarty, who lived across the road from her, then made for her front door. She opened it with the key that she had been allowed to have since her eleventh birthday, and stepped into the hallway.

The smell of baking wafted out from the kitchen, and even though Annie hadn't been hungry, she suddenly felt her mouth watering. She loved Ma's apple dumplings, and it would be a great way to celebrate her good news if that was what they were having tonight. There might even be extra helpings if her brothers Eamon and Sean were working late and eating at work. Although Annie was the youngest of seven, two of her sisters, Gert and Julia, had died as children, and Shay and Mary were married now, so that just left Eamon and Sean to share the house with Annie and her parents.

She entered the living room and was pleased to see Da sitting in the good armchair and reading the newspaper. Da worked long but irregular hours, driving people around the city in his hackney, a Model T Ford that was his pride and joy. One of the good points of the job, however, was that because he kept the car in a former stable just around the corner, he could often pop home for a quick cup of tea between fares.

He looked up at Annie now, over his reading glasses, and gave her a grin.

'So, how's me little scholar?'

'Great, Da. And eh ... could we get Ma? I've news.'

Her father took off his glasses and shot a quizzical look at Annie. 'The scholarship?'

Annie had planned to tell them both at the same time but she nodded happily to her father, unable to keep the smile from her face.

'Maura!' he called, and her mother came in from the kitchen, still wearing a flour- covered apron.

'What's going on?' she asked.

'Tell her, Annie,' prompted Da.

'I got the scholarship, Ma! I'm going to Eccles Street!'

'Oh, Annie. That's ... that's just great. Come here to me!'

Even though she was twelve now Annie didn't hesitate, and

she ran into her mother's arms like she used to do when she was smaller.

'Well done, pet … well done,' said Ma emotionally, and when she finally released her, Annie could see a tear in the corner of her mother's eye.

'You might as well give your aul' Da a hug too,' said her father.

Annie turned and happily embraced him.

'Well done, chicken,' he said. 'I don't know where you got the brains from, but you got them somewhere!'

'Thanks, Da.'

Her father had been smiling but now he looked serious and he reached out and placed a hand on Annie's shoulder.

'The first in our family, Annie. We're so proud of you. Ma and me, we're … we're just so proud.'

Annie felt a lump in her throat. She had known this would be important to her parents but she hadn't realised quite how deeply it would affect them. It moved her how much they were pleased for her, especially since she had recently overheard her father discussing money, and telling her mother how it was a struggle to repay the loan that he had had to take out to buy the Model T. She had never talked to her parents about money before – it just wasn't the kind of thing you did – but now she felt she ought to say something.

'I know…' she began, haltingly. 'I know that even with the scholarship … it still costs money to send me to Eccles Street. And I just … I really want to say thanks. Thanks so much for letting me go.'

'Oh, Annie,' said her mother.

'I won't let you down, Ma. Or you, Da. I know how hard you

work. And I promise … I promise I'll do my very best to make it worthwhile.'

Her father looked at her, and now there was a tear in his eye.

'You're one in million, Annie Reilly,' he said softly, then he put one arm around Ma and held out the other.

Annie could feel her own eyes welling up, and she swallowed hard, then wrapped herself in her parents' arms.

CHAPTER TWO

▬ ▬ ▬

Peter knew that Tommy was going to beat him. He was slightly better than his friend and neighbour at most sports, but today Tommy's eye was in, and Peter was sorry he had made a bet on volleying with a tennis ball. Tommy's father was the local vet, and the boys were in the field behind the rambling house that served both as a vet's surgery and the O'Neill family home. With their tennis rackets in hand they were competing to see who could hit the most volleys against the high boundary wall of the garden, without the ball touching the ground.

'Fifty!' cried Tommy, surpassing Peter's best score of forty-nine, then continuing in a relaxed groove and smoothly volleying back and forth.

'All right, all right,' said Peter with a wry grin, 'don't rub it in.'

'Once I get the steeler.'

The season for playing marbles was coming to a close, but the big metal marbles known as 'steelers' – in actual fact large ball-bearings – were still valuable possessions. Peter regretted his hastiness in betting one on his volleying skills, but there was no point being a bad loser, he thought, and he raised his hand in acceptance. 'Don't worry, I'll drop it over to you after tea.'

'Great.'

It was late on a warm May afternoon and Peter lay down onto the grass and let the sun shine on his face. Tommy caught the ball cleanly as a final volley rebounded off the wall, then he threw the ball and racket onto the grass and flopped down beside his friend.

'Did you hear the latest?' asked Tommy.

'What?'

'Dad says the army will have to storm the Four Courts. That they might even use artillery on the rebels.'

'Really?'

'Yeah.'

'God ...'

The anti-Treaty republicans had occupied the imposing buildings on Inns Quay known as the Four Courts, an action that was seen as a direct challenge to the new government. The city was rife with rumours, and Peter had heard a boy in school claiming that Michael Collins was under huge pressure to unleash the army against the republicans.

'What else did your dad say?' asked Peter.

'That he understands the rebels wanting to fight on, but that it's pointless.'

Peter found this really discouraging. He had always sensed that Mr O'Neill was the most nationalist of his friends' parents. And now even he seemed willing to give up the fight.

'It's not pointless,' he argued. 'People said that about taking on the British, and still we won in the end.'

'But this isn't the British. This is fighting other Irishmen.'

Pater sat up and looked at his friend. 'So do you think it's pointless too?'

Tommy continued lying back on the grass and shrugged.

'I don't know, Peter. I'm just telling you what my dad said.'

Peter was about to argue further but he stopped himself. He didn't want to fall out with Tommy. They were good friends who played rugby and tennis together, went to school together – even went together to an Irish language club. You couldn't say Tommy wasn't up for the republic, or that he was cowardly. In fact he was as a brave a scrum-half as Peter had played rugby with – but he was a follower rather than a leader, and Peter knew that he wouldn't change.

Besides, it might be wise not to show his own hand too much. If he was going to pursue his plan to get involved in the conflict, maybe it would be better to keep some things to himself. But how could he get involved? He had thought of going down to the Four Courts and asking to talk to some of the men occupying the buildings, but they would almost certainly treat him as a kid and not take him seriously. He would have to think of something, but for now it might be best to keep things normal with Tommy.

'Will we go down to Nugent's Field and light a fire?' he suggested. 'I can get some sausages.'

'Great!' said Tommy, sitting up enthusiastically, the conversation about the rebels already put behind him.

Peter was glad he hadn't taken the argument further with his friend. Tommy always avoided conflict, but other people had much stronger views, and as they made their way across the sunlit meadow, Peter knew that serious trouble was brewing.

* * *

'I heard a good school joke,' said Annie.

'What is it?' queried Josie Gogarty.

They were standing under a lamppost with a group of other girls, waiting their turn to skip with a long rope that was tied to the post. The sun was beginning to go down behind the cottages on St Josephine's Avenue, but the evening was still balmy and Annie felt relaxed.

'Did you hear about the cross-eyed teacher?' she asked.

'No,' said Josie.

'She couldn't control her pupils!'

The other girls laughed, and Annie was glad that she had memorised the joke, which she had seen in the children's page of Da's newspaper.

Josie was still smiling but now she turned to Annie. 'You won't have to worry about that, will you?'

'How do you mean?' asked Annie.

'In your new school. Easy to control those kids – yis would all be too posh to act up.'

A couple of the girls smiled at Josie's retort, and Annie was taken aback. The shift from laughter at her joke to being singled out as not one of the gang had come out of the blue. In one way, she wasn't all that surprised at Josie; even though she lived just across the road they had never been close friends. But nobody had come to Annie's defence, no one had said, 'Don't be silly, Annie's not stuck-up, she's one of us.'

Annie sensed that how she handled this would be important, and she thought for a moment, then looked Josie in the eye. 'You'll be working in the sewing factory when you leave school next year, won't you?'

'Yeah, what's wrong with that?'

'Nothing, because that's what you want,' said Annie, keeping her voice calm. 'Just like I'm going to secondary school because that's what I want. It doesn't make me posh or stuck-up. If you can do what you want, why shouldn't I?'

'Do what you want then,' said Josie dismissively before turning back to the skipping.

No one else said anything further, and the skipping game resumed, but Annie sensed that the mood was with Josie. It seemed unfair to be criticised in advance for possibly making friends in her new school with wealthier girls. Annie had always thought it was silly the way the children from better-off families didn't play with children of their own age who lived only a few roads away. But now she saw that her own friends were just as set in their thinking as the stuck-up kids that they didn't like.

Then it was her turn to skip the rope, and she stepped forward eagerly, knowing that she mustn't let the others think that she was rattled. She jumped enthusiastically while the other girls sang a skipping song. But even as she skipped she couldn't help thinking that winning the scholarship was going to be more complicated than she had imagined.

CHAPTER THREE

━━ ━━ ━━ ━━

Peter sang at the top of his voice, even though he wasn't a good singer. It didn't matter though, 'Peigín Leitir Móir' was the kind of song that it was fun to roar out even if you couldn't stay in tune. He was at the Irish language club that Tommy and his sister had joined at the suggestion of their father, Mr O'Neill, and it hadn't taken much persuading from Tommy to get Peter to join too.

The club was held in the drawing room of a big Georgian house in Gardiner Street. It encouraged children to speak Irish and provided opportunities for singing, drama, table tennis, chess and occasional outings. Apart from the club being fun, Peter was also attracted by the idea of learning to speak Irish more fluently. The vast majority of Dubliners spoke English as their native language, but many people who learnt Irish did so as a form of resistance to British culture, and it had been this notion that had made Peter suspect Mr O'Neill of being a secret nationalist.

His own parents had never been nationalists, but now that there was going to be an Irish Free State even people like Mam and Dad were having to adapt, and Peter had convinced his mother that it made sense for him to become fluent in Irish.

The next chorus of the song started, and Peter shouted out the catchy tune, winking at Tommy as they revelled in the rowdiness. He could see Mr McMahon, the club supervisor, smiling at their enthusiasm. Mr McMahon taught geography and maths in Belvedere, where he was seen as a tough but fair teacher; but in the Irish language club he was more relaxed. He looked around now, as the door to the room opened, then he nodded in greeting as another adult approached him.

McMahon had closely cropped ginger hair and was a heavily built man of about fifty. The second man was well built also, but much younger, probably in his late twenties. He approached Mr McMahon and shook hands, then discreetly handed him a large envelope. Peter had been singing along with gusto, but now he stopped abruptly. He stared at the younger man in disbelief. Then the man looked up, almost as if he sensed Peter staring, and their eyes met. Peter swallowed hard. There was no mistake. This was the gunman he had saved from the Black and Tans a year earlier. The man held his gaze for a second, then looked away.

Peter felt his pulses racing and he watched as the man spoke briefly to Mr McMahon, then made for the door. Peter waited to see if the man would look round at him again, but he didn't, leaving the room without a backward glance. It had all happened really quickly, but Peter was in no doubt. It was definitely the gunman. And what was more, the man had recognised him. He was certain of it.

The song came to an end, and Mr McMahon announced free time. This was when there was no organised activity, and the club members chatted with each other before everyone was served a glass of milk and a bun, and the club finished for the night.

Peter took a breath, willing himself to act. For ages he had dreamed about playing some part in fighting for a full republic, and this was his chance, if he could get up the nerve to go to Mr McMahon. The club supervisor must surely be a secret rebel if he was getting correspondence from a gunman, and Peter knew that he had to approach him. But McMahon was an adult, and a teacher in Peter's school, and he was nervous of confronting him. What was he going to say – *I know you're with the rebels?* The older man might get really angry. But if he didn't act now he might never get a chance like this again.

Before he knew what he was doing, he said 'back in a minute' to Tommy, then started towards the teacher, walking quickly before he lost his nerve.

'Peader,' said Mr McMahon, addressing Peter by the Irish version of his name.

'Mr McMahon,' said Peter, for once ignoring the Irish-speaking rule of the club, knowing that what he had to say would be difficult even in English. 'I know… I know who that man was. And *what* he is…'

McMahon raised a hand to interrupt him, but Peter ploughed ahead in a low voice, knowing that if he didn't spill it out now he never would. 'I know what you're doing, sir.'

McMahon looked taken aback, and, sensing that he had the teacher on the back foot, Peter continued, 'I know what's going on – and I'm on your side. Your friend will tell you how I saved him from the Tans. I want to help again. I know I'm too young to do the fighting, but I'll carry messages, I'll smuggle ammo, I'll be a runner. Please, don't just say no. You might be really glad of someone who can get through checkpoints as a schoolboy. Talk to your friend, sir, he'll tell you what I did.'

McMahon said nothing, his expression thoughtful, and Peter decided to go for broke, even if it involved a hint of blackmail.

'I want in, sir. And I don't mean to be rude, but I won't take no for an answer.'

* * *

Annie badly wanted to look like she fitted in, but she wasn't sure if she actually did. She was wearing her Sunday clothes, which she had always thought were really nice, but lots of the girls around her were more smartly dressed as they attended the welcome day in the assembly room of Eccles Street convent. It was a Saturday in early June, and she wouldn't be attending classes until the follow-ing September, but the nuns had arranged today's event to intro-duce all the incoming first years. Already some girls had looked at Annie appraisingly, and she couldn't help but feel that in their eyes she didn't quite pass the test. It was obvious, too, that girls who attended junior school here were at an advantage, and Annie had seen sub-groups forming of girls who clearly knew each other and were at ease.

The school itself looked imposing to Annie – bigger, more elaborate in its furnishings, and far better maintained than her local primary school. The corridors in Eccles Street all seemed to be highly polished and smelling of beeswax, and sunshine flooded in through spotless window panes. It was very impressive, but also a bit scary in that it appeared to suggest that anyone coming here had better be as perfect as the surroundings.

Annie's nervousness wasn't helped when a nun swept in, went

to the top of the room and clapped her hands loudly.

'Your attention, girls,' she said in a commanding voice, and immediately all conversation stopped. 'I'm Sister Immaculata, the Vice Principal of the school, and I'm here to welcome you all to Eccles Street.'

Annie was sitting about half way down the room, and she looked closely at the squat, middle-aged nun. Even though she was welcoming them, Annie reckoned that Sr Immaculata wasn't someone you would want to cross.

'I bet she's dead strict,' whispered the girl sitting next to Annie.

'I'd say so,' whispered Annie in return, and they exchanged a quick conspiratorial smile.

Annie had nodded in greeting when the girl had sat beside her a moment ago, but Sr Immaculata had come in before they could chat. Now, as the nun lectured them about the school's history and traditions, and how they would be expected to maintain the high standards of former pupils, Annie took in the other girl's appearance. She had shiny black hair that fell in curls, and dark brown eyes, and she wore a blue velvet dress with matching ribbons that Annie knew must have cost a lot of money. Suddenly the nun stopped speaking, and with a sense of panic Annie looked up, fearful that Sr Immaculata might have spotted Annie glancing at her neighbour.

To her relief Annie saw that she hadn't, and she realised that the nun had paused for emphasis, before continuing. 'You'll enter a different world when you come here in September,' she said. 'Your days as primary school children will be over, and you'll be taking the first steps on the road to becoming well-educated, well-mannered and pious young ladies. I should add that besides being

Vice-Principal I'll also be taking some of you for the subjects of Religious Doctrine and Mathematics.'

'Pray it's not us,' whispered Annie's neighbour again, and Annie wanted to smile, but held it back in case the nun might spot her.

'I'm sure at that stage we'll get to know each other better,' concluded Sr Immaculata. 'Meanwhile, we'll now have a tour of the school. Following the tour we shall reconvene here, at which stage I'll introduce you to Sister Josephine, who will be your Year Head. Form pairs, please, then follow me.'

Annie turned to the girl beside her. 'Will we be a pair?' she asked.

'Yes. What's your name?'

'Annie.'

'I'm Susie.'

Annie remembered her manners, and how Ma had told her to behave if she was introduced to anyone. 'How do you do, Susie?' she said, offering her hand.

Susie shook her hand and grinningly replied, 'How do you do, Annie?' then they looked at each other and suddenly laughed at the formality.

'Come on, then,' said Susie. They rose to follow Sister Immaculata, and Annie felt relieved that however intimidating Eccles Street was, it seemed now like she might get to face it with a friend.

* * *

'Couldn't you just eat lemon cake till you burst?' asked Susie happily.

Her mouth full, Annie nodded in agreement, for there was no denying that the home-made confectionery served by the nuns after the tour *was* delicious. They were back in the assembly room now, enjoying tea and cakes, having being shown round the school. Annie was more impressed than she had expected – the school even had its own chapel, a building that Annie thought was beautiful.

Attending Eccles Street was going to be very different from her old national school, with its leaking roof and smelly toilets, and Annie was excited about starting here in September. It would still be pretty nerve-racking being a new girl in a big school, but at least now she had chatted with several other girls during the tour, so she would know a few faces that first Monday morning.

And then there was Susie. The two girls had hit it off at once, and within minutes Annie had learnt that her new friend lived in Glasnevin with her parents and her twin brother Tommy, who attended Belvedere College. Susie attended primary school in the Holy Faith convent in Glasnevin, but her mother was sending her to Eccles Street next term because of a disagreement with the nun in charge of finance at the Holy Faith.

'It was gas!' Susie had explained. 'Mummy ran a bazaar to raise funds for the school, but Sister Regina – everyone calls her Mut-tonhead – fell out with Mummy over not paying the suppliers' bills fast enough.'

'Right. And don't you mind having to change schools?'

'Not really. Muttonhead would have had it in for me, so I'm well out of it. And Belvedere is only round the corner from Eccles Street, so I can travel each morning with Tommy – it'll be fun.'

Annie had sensed at once that Susie's family must be well off, but she decided to be honest with Susie from the start and not to pretend that her own family was any better off than it was. So she had told her new friend about living in St Alphonsus Avenue, and about Da driving the hackney, and Ma working part time as a milliner, and her two older brothers who lived at home and worked in the Hammond Lane foundry. If Susie was aware of the gap between their backgrounds it didn't seem to bother her, and in fact she had been dismissive of the haughty looking girls who were already forming their own little groups.

'Pity about them!' Susie said, when Annie had pointed out that some of them seemed a bit stuck-up.

'So, who have we got here?' said a soft country voice, and Annie turned round to face the speaker.

It was the other nun, Sr Josephine, who had been presented as their Year Head.

'I'm Annie Reilly, Sister.'

'I'm Susan O'Neill, Sister. But everyone calls me Susie.'

'Do they? Then Susie it will be,' said the nun with a smile. 'I presume, Annie, that's what everyone calls you – Annie?'

'Yes, Sister.'

'Right. Well, I'm glad we got that cleared up,' said Sr Josephine, and Annie noticed how her eyes seemed to twinkle when she smiled. It was hard to tell how old the nun was because she wore a full habit that exposed only her face, but she was younger and friendlier than Sr Immaculata, and Annie was glad that she was going to be their Year Head.

'And where do you live, Susie?'

'Brookville Lodge, Sister – in Glasnevin.'

'Very good. And you, Annie?'

'St Alphonsus Avenue, Sister.'

'Ah ... yes. I have you now, you're the scholarship girl.'

Annie experienced a sinking feeling. She had thought that Sr Josephine was going to be nice, with her smiling eyes and lilting country accent. Instead, the nun had made her feel different, like a charity case. She felt her cheeks colour and wasn't sure what to say. There was a brief awkwardness, then Susie bridged the gap.

'Annie is the brainbox all right,' she said cheerily, 'not like half the rest of us!'

Annie felt a surge of affection for her new friend, then she looked again at Sr Josephine, and to her surprise realised that the nun looked slightly uncomfortable.

'There's room for everyone, Susie,' said the nun, then she turned and looked directly at Annie. 'And every pupil is welcome. Very welcome indeed. I hope you'll be happy in Eccles Street. And I look forward to meeting you both in September.'

'Thank you, Sister,' replied the girls, then the nun moved off.

'I'd say she might be OK,' said Susie.

'Yes,' answered Annie, feeling that the nun had consciously tried to make up for embarrassing her.

'But we don't have to wait till September.'

'How do you mean?'

'To see each other,' said Susie enthusiastically. 'I'll ask Mummy if you can visit – I know she'll say yes. It's not that far from Drum-condra to Glasnevin.'

'Well ...'

'And we can play in our garden, or down in Nugent's Field with the boys. Say you'll come?'

'I'd ... I'd love to – if I'm allowed.'

'Tell them it's to do with school. That we're … that we're comparing booklists or something. Grown-ups always love you doing anything to do with school or classes.'

'OK.'

'And you could join our Irish club.'

'What's that?'

'It's a thing I'm in with Tommy and his friend Peter. It's supposed to improve our spoken Irish, but I'm really in it for the fun.'

'Where's it held?'

'In Gardiner Street. It's free, and we do games and lots of other stuff. And it runs on into the summer, so we could keep in touch.'

'Sounds great.'

'So, I'll ask my Mum, and you'll ask yours?'

Annie nodded in agreement. 'Definitely.'

'That just leaves one thing to do,' said Susie looking mischievously at the tea table.

'More lemon cake?' asked Annie with a grin.

'More lemon cake!' said Susie.

CHAPTER FOUR

━━ ━━ ━━ ━━

Peter felt bad as he walked down Church Street towards the quays. He had just passed a row of tenement houses outside of which scrawny children were playing. A strong smell of pee wafted out of the hallways, made worse by the warm summer sunshine. A little boy, his diseased legs misshapen by rickets, looked listlessly at Peter, and all of the children were filthy and hungry looking. Peter had just had a big Sunday lunch and was feeling full after a meal of pork steak, roast potatoes, cabbage, and rhubarb crumble.

It seemed really unfair to Peter that so many other people in Dublin hadn't enough to eat, and were packed like sardines into horrible, foul-smelling tenements, while his family should live comfortably. It wasn't his fault that his family was well off, but he still felt bad that things were so unjust, and he thought that these were the kind of conditions that should be changed in the new Irish Republic for which he wanted to fight.

Today would bring his first chance to play an active part, and he felt his heart beating faster at the thought. He reached the junction of Church Street and North King Street, the site where Kevin Barry had been arrested after shooting a British soldier a couple of years earlier during the War of Independence. As a former pupil of Belvedere, Kevin Barry's case had fascinated Peter, and he had been shocked when the eighteen-year-old rebel had been hanged in Mountjoy Jail. He hoped that if it came to it, he would be as brave as Barry had been, and the thought focused his mind on what he had to do today.

He transferred his rugby kit bag from one hand to the other, hoping that the football bag would make it clear that he was a schoolboy, the way it had a year ago when he had been stopped by the Black and Tans. But if he was stopped on his mission today and the bag thoroughly searched he would be in serious trouble.

His mission. The very words sent a shiver up his spine. But a mission is what it was, and he had been buzzing with anticipation ever since Mr McMahon had asked him to stay back after class a few days previously. The teacher had seemed annoyed when Peter insisted on getting involved with the republican movement on the night that the gunman had shown up at the Irish language club. McMahon had made it clear that he still wasn't happy with Peter's behaviour, but he had obviously had the Black and Tan incident confirmed by the gunman, and presumably they could see the value of a cool-headed schoolboy for getting around enemy security.

At any rate, Peter had been given an envelope for the commander of the Anti-Treaty forces occupying the Four Courts, and told to make certain that it was delivered safely. For all he knew the envelope might contain blank sheets of paper if they were being cautious and just trying him out, but either way this would count as a test, and he knew that if he did well it could lead to other operations.

First, though, he had to be successful today, and as he passed the

Fr Mathew Hall and the Capuchin Chapel at Church Street, Peter felt his anxiety rising even further.

The new government hadn't yet attempted to storm the Four Courts, but the complex could be under observation, and he knew that there was a risk involved in what he was about to try. But other people were taking risks, much bigger risks that cost them their lives. From his newspaper scrapbooks, he knew that over seventy people had been killed in Belfast the previous month in shootings between Irish nationalists and pro-British loyalists, so what he was about to do wasn't so daring, really. Even still, as he drew nearer the Four Courts, his mouth was dry with nervousness.

The main entrance was on the river side of the complex, on Inns Quay, and Peter had already decided that making for the front entrance was out of the question. Instead, he would turn left and approach from the rear at Chancery Street. But first he had to get past the Irish army troops who were clustered around a lorry parked at the kerb in Church Street.

The troops weren't actually cordoning off the road – it seemed that they were just establishing a presence in the area – but Peter still had to pass by them and it was important not to draw attention by appearing nervous. He walked nonchalantly along the pavement, then drew level with the soldiers. *Would he look shifty if he didn't make eye contact? Or would it be more of a mistake to stare at them and get noticed?* He decided to look at the soldiers with mild curiosity, then look away. Whistling a little tune as though lost in his own world, he passed by the troops. He half expected some kind of challenge. Then he told himself that this was because he knew what was in the bag, and that the soldiers probably just saw him as another schoolboy going to play in a match.

He turned, unchallenged, into Chancery Street, breathing out in relief. But he couldn't relax for long, because while Chancery Street backed onto the rear of the Four Courts, it also contained the Bridewell Police Station. Across the road he could see the barricaded windows behind which the rebels occupied the courts buildings, but there was nobody about on the street, which gave him hope. He walked on, forcing himself to keep his pace casual. Just as he drew near to the entrance to the Bridewell, a tall Dublin Metropolitan Policeman stepped out the door. Peter saw the DMP man quickly taking in his well-dressed appearance.

The man raised his hand in a signal to halt. 'You're not from round here, son, are you?'

'No,' said Peter striving to keep his voice normal. 'I'm from Glasnevin.'

The policeman pointed towards the barricaded building across the way. 'This isn't a great place to be. What are you doing down here?'

'Just taking a short cut on the way to a match.' Peter indicated the kitbag. 'I've a rugby game for Belvedere.' He held the policeman's gaze, sensing that an innocent person wouldn't feel the need to say any more.

The DMP man looked at Peter for a moment, and he felt his stomach tightening. Although the police would be careful in dealing with people as respectable as his parents, even Dad's standing as a professional man wouldn't save him now if the policeman discovered what was in the kitbag.

After a moment, the man seemed to reach a decision and he nodded. 'Enjoy your game. But you'd be safer cutting out onto the quays.' He pointed to the corner round which Chancery Place led towards the river Liffey.

'Right,' said Peter, 'I'll go that way.'

The policeman nodded again, then continued briskly towards Church Street. Peter moved slowly now, crossing the road towards the side of the Four Courts and glancing casually behind him. As soon as the DMP man was out of sight he walked more swiftly. There was nobody on the street now – he suspected most people were avoiding the vicinity of the occupied Four Courts – and this would be his best chance of succeeding.

He went quickly toward the side entrance that straddled the junction of Chancery Street and Chancery Lane and saw that the gate was heavily barricaded and manned by two armed rebels. Peter quickly began to open the kitbag and both men immediately trained their rifles on him.

'It's OK,' he said reassuringly, 'it's OK. Orders for the Officer in Command.'

The men looked taken aback, and Peter continued, adopting a confidence that he didn't really feel: 'This is to go to the Officer in Command, at once.' He reached down into the middle of his rugby gear, then withdrew a rolled up envelope and passed it through the gate.

One of the men took the envelope, and Peter said 'Up the Republic!' Then he swiftly closed his kitbag, looked around to make sure the street was still deserted, and started walking towards the quays.

★ ★ ★

Annie sat nervously in the kitchen pretending to read the children's section of Da's Sunday paper. She wanted to find the right words to tell her parents about Susie's invitation to visit her home. On returning from Eccles Street yesterday all the family had been full of questions, and Annie had told them excitedly about the school, and the nuns, and some of the girls she had met. But she hadn't disclosed that Susie had invited her to Glasnevin, sensing somehow that it would be better to leave that until later. Now, though, she felt that having to raise the subject on its own was going to make it seem important. And it would be really disappointing if her parents forbade her to visit the first friend she had made in her new school. *She had to get this right.*

Eamon and Sean were out at a football match, so she had her parents to herself, and she was rehearsing in her mind the kind of casual voice she might use in asking permission, when her father rose from the kitchen table.

'I better make a start,' he said.

'I did some sandwiches, Jim, they're in the breadbin,' said her mother.

'Are you working, Da?' asked Annie in surprise. Her father put in long hours driving the hackney, but usually he took Sundays off.

'Have to take some big-wig in from Sutton to the Department of Finance,' he answered.

'On a Sunday?'

'The country's in a crisis, Annie. The government can't just work office hours – and neither can I.'

'No. And I'm … I'm sorry, Da.'

'For what?'

'Well, my new school is going to cost so much, with uniforms and all.'

'Don't worry your head about that, Annie,' said Ma. 'We're just delighted that you're getting the chance.'

'And we'll have you looking as smart as any of them. We'll earn whatever it takes.'

'Thanks, Da,' said Annie, touched. 'Thanks, Ma.'

Her mother smiled, and Annie decided to take the plunge. 'There's something else I wanted to ask you,' she said.

'What's that?' replied Ma.

'You remember I said I met some girls at the convent,' continued Annie, trying to keep her tone casual. 'One of them, Susie O'Neill is her name, asked could I come up to her house to visit.'

Ma looked at her with interest. 'Where does she live?'

'Glasnevin.'

'Whereabouts in Glasnevin?' queried Da.

'Botanic Road.'

'It's not O'Neill the vet, is it?' said Da.

'Yes, she said her father's a vet.'

Da looked uncertain. 'They're a bit …'

'What?'

'A bit law-dee-daw for us maybe.'

'No, Da, Susie is lovely. She's dead friendly, not a bit stuck-up – you'd like her.'

'I'm sure I would. But still …'

Annie looked at her father in dismay. It was bad enough that her friends on the road had closed minds and thought that no one should play with anyone unless they were from exactly the same neighbourhood. But now Da seemed to be thinking the same way.

'We're just looking out for you, love,' said her mother. 'Susie might be nice, but maybe her people … well they might look down a bit on us.'

'Why would they? We're as good as anyone else.'

'I know that, love, and you know that,' said Da. 'But other people mightn't think that way.'

'How can that ever change if everyone stays apart?' asked Annie. She saw that her parents didn't have a ready answer, and she pushed on. 'Please, let me be friends with her. If it doesn't work out I won't go again. But let me try at least.'

Annie watched anxiously as Da looked to Ma for a decision. Her mother hesitated briefly, then nodded. 'All right, love. Visit her if you like – but just don't be too disappointed if … well, if everything doesn't work out.'

'I won't. And thanks for letting me go,' said Annie, then she rose and made for the door, relieved, but still a bit disappointed with her parents' reaction.

✳ ✳ ✳

'You're a right little glutton, aren't you?' said Peter's older brother John, as the family enjoyed their Sunday tea in the sunlit dining room.

'What's it to you if I've more crumble?' retorted Peter

'You won't stay on the rugger team if you've a big fat belly.'

'John!' admonished their mother 'Don't be vulgar, and don't tease.'

Out of sight of their mother, Peter made a face at his older brother. He hated the way he talked down to him. Just because John was twenty and a university student he tried to adopt a man-of-the-world attitude that Peter found infuriating. Their father had just been called to the dental surgery for an emergency extraction, and in his absence John was acting like the man of the house.

Their sister Mary moved now to make the peace, as she often did, and she turned to Peter.

'Did you have a match this afternoon?' she asked. Mary's life revolved around music, which she taught in the nearby Holy Faith convent, and she had little interest in rugby. Still, she meant well, so Peter answered politely.

'No, I, eh…' Peter thought about his mission to the Four Courts, and he imagined their faces if they knew what he had really been doing, but of course he couldn't tell the truth. 'I went into the Bots with Tommy for a while,' he answered instead. 'The Bots' was slang for the adjacent Botanical Gardens, where the river Tolka flowed through many acres of landscaped grounds. There were exotic trees and plants, and large, tropically warm green-houses, and because it was an adventure land for local children Peter reckoned this was a convincing answer.

His mother, however, looked at him questioningly.

'I thought the O'Neills were visiting relatives in Rathgar?' she said.

Peter was caught unawares and he hesitated. 'Eh, yes, they … they were, later on,' he improvised, 'so Tommy couldn't stay for too long.'

'Right.'

His mother seemed satisfied with the explanation, but Peter realised that he'd have to be more careful. If he went on further missions for the rebels, as he hoped to, then he would need to have convincing stories prepared.

His brother began lecturing them now, going on importantly about diabetes, for which, he explained, a cure had been discovered in Canada. As John told them about something called insulin, his mother and Mary listened attentively – in Peter's opinion they were far too respectful of his standing as a medical student – but for once, he didn't mind as it gave him a chance to think things out. He would have to talk to Tommy, to make sure he would back up the story about the Bots, just in case it might arise in conversation with his mother. He would also have to come up with some explanation for Tommy as to why he misled his mother, but that should be all right, he would think of something. And anyway, Tommy wasn't the type to quiz him too closely.

He hadn't realised it would all be so complicated when he had approached Mr McMahon. But he wanted to play his part, he *had* to. He thought back to the hungry-looking children he had passed outside the tenement that afternoon. It wasn't that he hadn't seen real poverty before – it was rampant in many parts of Dublin – but somehow today he had linked their situation to his own actions. Forming a new republic shouldn't just be about changing a British government for an Irish one. The republic should be a place where there weren't any filthy, hungry children. That was worth fighting for, he reckoned, and whatever the risks, he was going to take them.

CHAPTER FIVE

'Come on and we'll annoy the boys!' said Susie.

Annie followed her new friend out through the French windows, curious to meet Susie's twin brother, Tommy, and eager to explore the O'Neill's extensive back garden. Annie's house had no garden, just a yard in the back where Ma kept her beloved potted plants, but Susie's home had trimmed lawns, mature trees, a high stone boundary wall and lots of interesting nooks and crannies. The house itself was an imposing granite building, with a portico over the front door and ivy growing on the walls. Annie had been impressed by its grandeur – which Susie clearly took for granted – but she had been careful not to sound too overawed, not wanting to emphasise the difference in their backgrounds.

On her arrival, Annie had met Mrs O'Neill, but hadn't yet seen Mr O'Neill who was delivering a foal at a farm in Ashtown. Annie had been a little nervous about meeting Susie's mother, but, as it turned out, Mrs O'Neill was like an older version of Susie, with a quick smile and flashing eyes. She was expensively dressed and well spoken, but she had offered the girls lemonade, and had put Annie at her ease and made her feel welcome.

Now Annie followed Susie as she strode towards a corner of

the garden in which a home-made swing had been tied to the bough of a large tree. A boy with dark hair and brown eyes – obviously Susie's twin – was being vigorously pushed on the swing by another, taller boy with wavy fair hair.

'Halt in the name of the law!' said Susie, jumping in front of her brother and bringing the swing to a juddering stop by grabbing the rope.

'You're such a messer, Susie!' cried the dark-haired boy.

'Mind your manners. I want you to meet my friend.'

Annie smiled, hoping the boy wouldn't be too annoyed at having his fun cut short by her introduction. To her relief he smiled back.

'I'm Tommy,' he said.

Annie had been warned by her mother to behave correctly today and had shaken hands and said 'How do you do?' when meeting Mrs O'Neill. But now she copied Tommy's informality and simply responded, 'Hello, I'm Annie.'

'And this big galoot is Peter Scanlon,' said Susie.

'You're heading for a ducking in the Tolka,' threatened the other boy, but he grinned as he said it, and Annie could see that he wasn't offended.

'Hello, Peter,' she said. 'Annie Reilly.'

Peter gave her a friendly nod. 'Anything to Simon Reilly?'

'Eh, no … I don't think so.'

'He's in Belvedere with us,' said Peter. 'His dad's a barrister. I thought you might be related.'

'No, we've no barristers in our family.' She left it at that. Even though Susie was completely unsnobbish herself, Annie didn't want to risk embarrassing her in front of the others by revealing that her father was a hackney driver, or that Eamon was a carter and Sean an apprentice fitter. No sooner had she thought this than Annie felt a stab of guilt. Her family was the most important thing in her life and she shouldn't have to hide her background. But before she got a chance to say anything further Susie chipped in.

'Simon Reilly – isn't he the boy with awful breath?'

'Yeah,' answered Tommy. 'When he sang in the Christmas show, the other boys asked for gas masks!'

'You should send him to your dad, Peter, get all his rotten teeth out,' said Susie.

'I wouldn't wish Simon Reilly on anyone,' answered Peter with a smile.

'Yeah, it must be horrible being a dentist,' said Susie wrinkling her face in distaste as she turned to Annie. 'Can you imagine working in people's smelly mouths?'

'No thanks,' said Annie. 'No offence to your father, Peter,' she added hastily, not feeling she knew the other boy long enough to be critical of his father's career.

'That's all right,' said Peter. 'I'd hate it too. Though my brother John says: "Dentistry is vital in the overall health of the individual."' He mimicked his brother in a really pompous voice, and Annie laughed with the others.

'I suppose loads of jobs have bad bits,' said Tommy. 'Remember Dad telling us about the cat with the glass in its paw? He was taking the glass out and the cat peed right into his face!'

'Yuck,' said Annie with a laugh

'But I'd still like to be a vet,' said Tommy. 'You can't let one bad thing put you off.'

'Yes you can,' said Susie. 'Stuff like that is always happening to vets.'

'So you don't want to be one?' asked Annie.

'God, no! Unless you really like it, why do the same job as your parents?'

Annie realised that this was a chance to raise her father's occupation naturally, and she spoke up. 'Yeah, my Da drives a hackney – I wouldn't like that job.'

'What car does he drive?' asked Peter

'A Model T Ford.'

Peter raised an eyebrow in appreciation. 'Driving that could be good.'

'But even worse things happen to drivers than having cats pee on you,' said Annie.

'Like what?' queried Susie.

'Last year Da was driving a man and he had a heart attack and died in the back seat.'

'That must have been awful,' said Tommy.

'Especially if he didn't pay the fare!' added Peter.

'Peter!' said Susie, laughingly admonishing him.

'That's the thing, he didn't!' said Annie. 'And when the man's brother came to thank Da for driving him to the hospital he still didn't pay the fare. Know what he said?'

'What?' asked Susie eagerly.

Annie adopted an exaggerated Dublin accent. 'The blessings of God on you, mister!'

The others laughed, then Susie said: 'Do you want a go on the swing?'

'OK – if that's all right?' said Annie, turning to Tommy.

'Yeah, you're grand,' he answered, sliding off the make-shift swing.

'And after that we could show Annie the steppiers,' said Peter.

'What's that?'

'Stepping stones down at the Tolka,' said Susie.

'We have races there,' explained Peter, 'if you're on for that.'

Annie was pleased at having been accepted without fuss by Susie's gang and she looked at the two boys and grinned. 'Yeah, I'm on for it – if you don't mind being beaten by a girl!'

✳ ✳ ✳

Peter was impressed, despite himself. When Annie had spoken earlier of being beaten by a girl he had treated it as a joke, but now as he watched her progress over the stepping stones he realised that she *was* fast. Like the others, she had taken off her shoes and socks in case she slipped into the shallow river, but her balance was excellent and when she completed the trip over the stones and back to their starting point, Susie called out: 'Nine seconds!'

'Nice stepping, Annie,' said Tommy, 'you'd make a good winger!'

'The highest praise there is from these lads!' said Susie, and Peter noted how Annie smiled, obviously pleased with the praise.

'That's putting it up to you, Peter,' said Susie, turning back to him.

'Nine seconds – less the handicap of two seconds you offered Annie,' said Tommy.

Susie had taken thirteen seconds and Tommy ten, so Peter reckoned if he beat seven now he would be the winner. 'No problem,' he said confidently, though in fact he knew that he would have to move really well to beat seven seconds.

'Ready?' asked Susie.

'Yes.'

'Good luck,' said Annie smilingly, and Peter wasn't sure if she meant it or if she was being tongue-in-cheek.

'One, two, three – go!' cried Susie.

Peter moved off at speed, jumping from rock to rock, then he reached the furthest point, swivelled, and leapt back in the direction from which he had started. He was doing well and felt that he had a chance of winning, when suddenly his foot slipped on one of the rocks. He threw his arms up instinctively to try and keep his balance, and for a second he seemed to hang poised. Then he landed, his bare feet splashing heavily down into the water.

He heard a derisive cheer from Susie and Tommy, and he waded in from the shallows as the others all laughed. He grinned ruefully, knowing that he had been beaten fair and square. As he gained the bank, Susie playfully announced: 'And today's winner is – Annie Reilly!'

Annie looked at him, her smile half apologetic. 'I'm sorry for laughing, Peter, it's just that you really reminded me of Coco.'

'Coco?'

'The clown. We went to see the circus and this clown called Coco kept losing his balance.' Annie did a quick impersonation, her arms flailing in a way that Peter realised must have been similar to his own efforts to keep his balance.

Annie grinned, but somehow Peter felt that she was laughing with him rather than at him and he found himself grinning back.

'OK', he said, 'no argument. You're the winner – this time.'

'Thanks,' said Annie, then she looked at him seriously. 'And can I just say one thing?'

'What?'

'The blessings of God on ye!'

The others laughed again, and Peter found himself joining in. He didn't know much about Susie's new friend, but already he sensed that Annie Reilly would be interesting.

CHAPTER SIX

▬▬ ▬▬ ▬▬

Peter had his scrapbook on the kitchen table and was eagerly cutting out stories from the newspapers that he had spread across the table. It was great to live at a time when there was so much going on.

'Well, Peter, what's happening in the world?' asked his father good-humouredly as he entered the room.

'Brilliant stuff, Dad.'

'Glad someone's found a bit of good news,' said his father with a smile.

Peter was pleased to see him relaxed; it was probably because it was Wednesday, and his father was looking forward to his game of golf.

'Look at this,' said Peter, 'the very same week that Amundsen sets off again for the North Pole, Mallory's team is trying to climb Mount Everest without oxygen.' Peter pointed to the stories, and a striking press photograph of the explorer Amundsen setting off for the Pole from the city of Seattle.

'Exciting stuff,' said his father.

'I'd love to go on a trip like that,' said Peter.

'Which one would you prefer?'

Peter considered. 'I'd say the North Pole. You could race across the snow pulled by huskies!'

'Right.'

'How about you, Dad?'

'On balance, I think I'll stick to the golf!' said his father with a grin. 'What else have you cut out?'

'Eh … there's a piece about the rebels in the Four Courts,' said Peter. Even though his father couldn't know about his recent mission there, Peter still felt a little nervous in mentioning the place.

'That's a bad business,' said his father, all amusement suddenly gone. 'The government should root them out.'

'But that would mean Irishmen fighting other Irishmen.'

'That's what these diehards trade on, Peter. They think just because they're Irish they can defy the government. It's madness.'

'How is it madness, Dad?'

'They've this half-baked notion that if they force a response from the British troops that haven't left yet, it would unite all Irishmen.'

'But wouldn't it be good for Irishmen to be united?' asked Peter.

'Yes, in the Free State we've been granted under the Treaty.'

'But the oath, Dad. They'd have to swear allegiance to the king of England.'

'They could do it under protest, on the grounds that it means nothing to them.'

'That's … that's like lying, though.'

'No, it's compromising, Peter. In a situation like this, nobody gets all the things they want.'

Although knowing that that he probably shouldn't alert his father to how strongly he felt, Peter couldn't help himself. 'But it's against everything they fought for!'

His father looked at him, and when he spoke again it was in the quiet tone that meant he was really serious. 'They got the bulk of what they fought for – an Irish Free State. All sensible people can see that. Be careful what you say on these matters, Peter. Even as a schoolboy you don't want to be heard saying the wrong thing. Do you understand?'

'Yes, Dad.'

But if everyone had been sensible there would have been no War of Independence – and they'd still be under British rule, he thought. But he didn't say that. Quite a lot of people had been happy enough with British rule. Even his own parents had regarded it as civilised and well intentioned. But Peter couldn't accept that it was right, and his heart was still with the rebels. In future he would have to be more careful in front of his father, but that would be just for show – because no matter what Dad said, he wasn't changing sides.

* * *

Annie was getting worried. She had arranged to meet Susie and Tommy outside the Irish language club in Gardiner Street, but there was no sign of them. Susie had suggested that they meet a few minutes early, and had promised to introduce her to some of the other members before the club began, but there wasn't going to be time for that now. Annie looked anxiously up the street, its tall Georgian buildings bathed in the evening sunshine, but there was no sign of the twins. There was no sign of their neighbour, Peter, either, and Annie felt nervous about joining a group of total strangers if none of her new friends showed up.

Annie was surprised that Susie wasn't here as arranged. After all, it had been Susie who had urged her to join the club, as they had made their way back to the O'Neill's house after their races at the stepping stones a couple of days previously. Annie had really enjoyed spending time with Susie, and meeting Tommy and Peter had been fun too, and she had arrived home in good spirits.

Ma had asked lots of questions, and Annie had said that Susie's family was very nice and friendly, and had downplayed the size of their house, and their obvious affluence. She could tell that Ma was relieved it had all gone well, and so it hadn't been hard to persuade her mother to let her to join the Irish language club.

Now, though, she was growing anxious, then she saw a figure turning the corner and advancing. It was Peter, and she smiled as he drew near.

'Annie,' he said in greeting.

'Hello, Peter.'

'Susie asked me to say she's really sorry. A pipe burst and flooded their kitchen. She and Tommy have to help in the clean-up, so she can't make it.'

'Oh, that's a pity.'

'Yeah, but they'll only miss tonight. Don't worry, I'll give your name to Mr McMahon.'

'Who's he?'

'The man in charge of the club. He's a teacher in our school. He's sound, you'll like him.'

'OK.'

Annie was glad that at least she would have Peter to introduce her, though she would still have preferred to have Susie, as another girl, to show her round on her first night in the club.

'Ah, Scanlon,' said a stocky boy who arrived at the doorway of the club with two companions. 'Who's your judy?'

Annie looked at the three boys, slightly embarrassed at the suggestion that she was Peter's girlfriend. The newcomers were around the same age as herself, and she could tell from their clothes that they were all from comfortable backgrounds.

'This is Annie Reilly,' said Peter. 'She's a friend of Susie O'Neill.'

He turned back to Annie and indicated the boys by way of introduction.

'Doyle, Maguire and Nelson.'

'Hello, lads,' said Annie, trying for a friendly tone.

'Well, hello Annie,' said Doyle, the stocky-looking boy, with a hint of mockery.

'Haven't seen you around,' said Maguire, 'where are you from?'

'Drumcondra.'

'Whereabouts?' asked Nelson.

'St Alphonsus Avenue.'

'The little backstreet up past the train station?' asked Doyle.

'It's near the station,' answered Annie.

'I took a wrong turn up there once,' said Doyle, 'but I got out fast!' He laughed unpleasantly, and the other two boys joined in.

'And that's where you live?' he asked with mock disbelief.

'Yes, it is,' said Annie, trying hard not to sound defensive.

'What's it to you where she lives?' said Peter.

Doyle looked at him with surprise, and Peter drew slightly nearer to him.

'What's her address got to do with joining the club?'

'Well, nothing maybe, but…'

'Then what are you going on about?'

Annie sensed that the stocky boy was probably a bully by nature and she hoped that Peter wouldn't get drawn into a fight on her behalf.

The other boy held Peter's gaze, then he shrugged as though none of this was important.

'Just a joke, Scanlon, relax. Come on, lads,' he said to his companions, and the trio turned away and entered the doorway of the club.

Annie was relieved. She realised that Peter was probably looked up to as a boy who was strong and a regular member of Belvedere's rugby team, and she was glad that he had been there to support her.

'Sorry about that,' said Peter.

'It's OK. And thanks.'

'You're grand. Oops, here's Mr Mac,' said Peter, indicating a heavy-set man who had come around the corner. 'Irish only, once he arrives, OK?'

'OK.'

'Fancy a game of table tennis?'

'If you don't mind another beating from a girl,' said Annie playfully.

'We'll see about that!' answered Peter, then he turned and made for the door.

Annie followed him, but despite her playful tone she was a little thrown by the incident with the boys. She wouldn't always have someone like Peter to defend her, and the more she spread her wings, the more there seemed to be people willing to put her down. *Would it be like that in Eccles Street too?* Probably, she thought glumly, then she pulled herself together. Starting school in Eccles

Street was months away, there was no point worrying about it now. Meanwhile, she would try not to let anyone get her down, and make the best of everything that came her way. Feeling a little better, she took a deep breath, then followed Peter into the club.

CHAPTER SEVEN

▬ ▬ ▬ ▬

'Sit down, Peter, and act like we're just fishing.' Mr McMahon indicated the flattened grass of the canal bank, and Peter lowered his bicycle, then sat beside the teacher. He opened a bait box and began to assemble his fishing rod. They were a little downstream from the third lock of the Royal Canal in Phibsboro, and being a sunny Saturday afternoon, there were plenty of people walking the towpath, while other fisherman were scattered at intervals along the waterway.

Mr McMahon had made no reference to Peter's mission of the previous Sunday when they met at the Irish club on Thursday night, but he had invited Peter to join him for some fishing this afternoon, and Peter was excited at the idea of getting further missions.

It had been a good week all round, he thought, what with delivering the letter to the Four Courts, making a new friend in Annie, getting her signed up as a member of the Irish club – and then beating her at table tennis!

As he assembled his rod, he looked across the still waters of the canal at the high walls of the nearby Mountjoy Prison. *Had McMahon picked this spot deliberately to spook him?* The jail certainly looked forbidding, and Peter was aware that it was inside its boundary walls that his fellow Belvedere pupil Kevin Barry had been executed. But if McMahon was testing his nerve by meeting so close to the prison, he was wasting his time. Peter was eager to be involved and he wasn't going to be scared off.

He had learnt his lesson, however, about being careful at home. Unlike the last time, when he had almost been caught in a lie, today he had been cautious. He had told his mother that he felt like going fishing for a while. His mother was in good form, having done well at bridge the night before, and she didn't quiz him further, but wished him luck with his angling.

He cast his baited line out onto the waters, keeping it well away from the teacher's line. It broke the sparkling surface of the sunlit water, and Peter held the rod comfortably and sat back. Neither of them said anything at first, then McMahon spoke, not looking directly at Peter, but instead gazing out across the canal.

'Well done last week,' he said.

'Thanks,' answered Peter, trying not to let his pleasure show too much.

'There might be some more jobs, if you're interested.'

'I am, definitely.'

'But it's not a game, Peter,' said McMahon warningly.

'I know that.'

'Do you?'

'Yes.'

'Do you know what can happen behind those walls?' the teacher said, indicating the towering stone walls of the jail. 'Do you know that any of us who are caught could end up there?'

Despite himself, Peter felt a tiny stab of fear – the prison really *did* look scary. But he had already decided that he was willing to take risks, so he kept his voice steady as he answered the teacher.

'I know that, sir. But it's not going to stop me.'

McMahon looked him directly in the eye, then nodded approvingly. 'Sound lad.'

Peter felt a surge of pride; from McMahon, this was high praise.

'Two other things, Peter, if we're working together. One, never approach me again at the club about any of this. When we want you, we'll make contact. OK?'

'Yes, sir.'

'And the second thing is crucial. I mentioned it before but now I'm going to spell it out. You don't *ever, ever* whisper a word of this. To *anyone.*'

'I wouldn't.'

'Not to your brother, not to your best friend – no one.'

'I understand.'

'You need to, Peter. Because if you reveal anything, it affects people's safety. Including your own. *Especially* your own. Do you know what I'm saying?'

Peter swallowed hard, realising that he was being threatened. It came as a shock, but then he thought that this was something that would have to be said to every volunteer. And it made sense. In fact it was actually exciting, because it meant that he was now being taken seriously, that the things he would do were important. 'Yes, I know what you're saying, sir. And you needn't worry.'

'Good man. We'll fish away here for a while, then you head off.'

'Right. And … when's my next job?'

'Tomorrow. Do you know the Tolka valley at Cardiffs Bridge?'

'Yes.'

'There's a package in my bait box. Deliver it to Willow Cottage.

It's up a laneway to the left of the bridge. Slip the package in your own bait box when you're leaving, all right?'

'Right.'

Just then Peter felt a pull on the line – he had hooked a fish. It seemed like a good omen and, excited by how things were going, he began reeling in the line.

★ ★ ★

Annie loved the scent of apple tarts baking. If she had to pick one smell that conjured up home this would definitely be it. It reminded her of when she was small and Ma used to let her use a leftover scrap of pastry to make the letter A, which Annie would place on top of the apple tart before it went in the oven. Now that she was twelve she didn't do that any more, but she still liked baking with her mother. She particularly enjoyed it when, like now, it involved just the two of them together in the kitchen, with Da and her brothers out at work.

Susie was coming for tea, and Ma had the house looking spic and span for the first visit of her new friend. The good china had been set on the table, and even though Annie didn't want too much of a fuss, she was still grateful that Ma wanted to make an effort on her behalf. Her mother had been encouraging also when a letter had arrived from Eccles Street convent. The vice-principal, Sister Immaculata, had outlined how the school was run, and the nuns' ambitions for their pupils, and she had included booklists and details of what Annie would need in order to take part in school sports and elocution lessons.

The letter had confirmed that Sister Josephine would be their year head, and Annie had explained to her mother that she was the younger nun that Susie and she had met at the induction day, and that she seemed nice, and less strict than Sister Immaculata.

'That all sounds great, Annie,' Ma had said. 'And elocution lessons, if you don't mind,' she added with a grin, 'you'll be the right lady!'

Annie had smiled in response, but in truth she felt a bit uneasy. She was excited at the idea of starting in Eccles Street, but she worried about moving into a new environment. Supposing that with elocution classes and well-off friends like Susie and Peter her family came to see her as different? It wasn't that they would mean to. But people *did* tend to treat you differently when you made any kind of change, and only yesterday it had caused a run-in with Josie Gogarty, when Annie had been returning with messages from the shop around the corner.

'If it isn't Annie Reilly,' Josie had said with a smirk. 'Or should I say Lady Muck? I thought you'd have servants getting your messages.'

Josie had been making snide remarks ever since the announcement about the scholarship, and Annie was tired of it. Up until now Annie had mostly let it go, not wanting to fall out with the other girls on the road. This time, though, she decided to make a stand. She remembered how Peter had taken a firm line with the bully who mocked her at the Irish club, and she put down the shopping bag and looked Josie straight in the eye.

'Can I ask you a question, Josie?' she said calmly.

'What?'

'Are you angry at yourself because you're thick? Or are you angry at me because I won a scholarship and you didn't?'

Josie's face flushed, and Annie could see that the other girl was furious. But now Josie was on her own, and without the back-up of her friends she seemed unsure how to respond.

'You think … you think you're someone, don't you?' she said finally.

'Everyone is someone, Josie.'

'You think you're so smart.'

'Smart enough to go to Eccles Street – and I won't apologise to you for it. And if you don't like that, take a running jump at yourself!' Annie picked up her shopping bag and turned on her heel, leaving Josie dumbstruck.

It had been a satisfying victory at the time, although Annie knew that she had definitely made an enemy.

Now, however, she sat with her mother in the kitchen, all the cooking in hand as they awaited their guest.

Ma turned to her.

'Annie?'

'Yes.'

'I just want to say… your da and I are delighted you've made new friends already. And … well I know we don't normally say this, but …' Her mother hesitated, trying to find the right words.

'What, Ma?'

'We're just … we're just so proud of you, pet.'

Annie felt a surge of affection for her mother and she reached out and squeezed her hand. 'Thanks, Ma,' she answered, then the knocker on the front door sounded, and she rose excitedly to her feet. 'That will be Susie!' she cried, and she made for the hall, her earlier worries forgotten as she went to welcome her friend.

CHAPTER EIGHT

■ ■ ■ ■

'Here's a brilliant riddle,' said Susie. '*I run but I never walk, I've a mouth but I never talk, I've a bed but I never lie – what am I?*'

'A pest,' answered Peter, lying back in the grass with his eyes closed against the strong June sunshine. He had gone for a picnic in the Tolka valley near Cardiffs Bridge with Tommy, Susie and Annie, and they had laid down their bicycles at a sheltered spot in one of the sloping fields leading down to the river.

'Give us a clue,' said Annie eagerly, and Peter smiled to himself, confirmed in his view that Annie would be competitive in every-thing she did. But she was a good sport too, and had taken her defeat in good grace when he had beaten her at table tennis the night she had joined the Irish club.

'All right, a clue then,' said Susie. 'Let's see…'

'Make it a good one,' said Tommy, 'it's too hot for frying our brains.'

'OK, this thing in the riddle – there's one near us right now.'

'Near us?' said Peter sitting up. He pointed at Susie. 'A head case?'

'You're hilarious!' she retorted, grabbing a handful of grass and throwing it at him.

'Say the riddle again' said Annie.

'*I run but I never walk, I've a mouth but I never talk, I've a bed but I never lie – what am I?*'

'Is it a dog?' asked Tommy.

Susie looked at her brother quizzically.

'How could it be a dog?'

'Well there's a dog outside one of the cottages down there at the bridge,' said Tommy, pointing. 'And dogs have mouths but they don't talk.'

'But they walk,' said Annie.

'Well, a lot of the time they run,' argued Tommy.

'And what about *I've a bed but I never lie*?' asked Susie.

'Dogs don't have beds, they sleep in kennels.'

'Ah for God's sake! You're not going to get it, are you?' said Susie. 'It's a river!'

'A river? Oh, that's a good one,' said Annie, 'though we might have got it, if you hadn't said.'

'And we might have ham sandwiches if we had ham – if we had bread!' said Peter, quoting one of his father's favourite sayings.

'We've something much better than ham sandwiches, haven't we, Annie?' asked Susie, the riddle suddenly forgotten as she pointed enthusiastically at their picnic bags.

'Well, for people who like apple tart,' said Annie.

'Doesn't everyone?' queried Susie. 'And this is the best apple tart you've ever tasted. I was down in Annie's yesterday, and her mother is a brilliant cook! And dead generous too, she made me take home a whole tart.'

Peter could see that Annie was pleased at Susie's praise, and he raised his hands as though in surrender.

'OK, forget the imaginary sandwiches! It's Mrs Reilly's apple tart!'

Annie smiled, and Peter was glad that she was with them today. In the short time since they had met, he had grown to like her, and she fitted well into their group, even if her background caused the occasional awkwardness.

There had been a brief moment of embarrassment earlier when they were preparing to set off from his house on the picnic. It was several miles from his home in Glasnevin to the countryside around Cardiffs Bridge, and the others had all agreed that it would be best to travel on their bicycles. Annie had had to admit that she had walked to Glasnevin, not having a bicycle, and Peter had seen his mother's surprise at Annie's confession. His mother had been slightly over-polite to Annie, as she sometimes was when dealing with people she thought of as social inferiors, but the moment passed quickly, and Peter suggested that Annie borrow his sister Mary's old bike, which had solved the problem.

He looked at his friends now, as Susie instructed Tommy to stoke up the campfire that they had lit with fallen wood. They didn't drink tea very often at home. But it was part of the fun of a picnic to make tea over an open fire, and so they had brought a sealed, metal billy-can full of water, to be boiled on the burning wood.

Peter's plan actually depended on the water, but as he watched the others, he felt slightly guilty about using them as cover on his mission. At the same time, it did make sense. If he had travelled alone to deliver Mr McMahon's package to the nearby cottage the chances were that no one would have paid too much heed to him. But by travelling as part of a group of kids having a picnic it definitely looked that bit more innocent and natural.

Now he just had to create an excuse to visit the cottage, and as Susie and Tony busied themselves with the fire, Peter rose and crossed to the billy-can, prising off its tight-fitting lid.

He stepped forward, casually holding the container in his right hand, then he deliberately tripped up.

'Damn,' he cried, falling awkwardly and dropping the billy-can as he used his hands to break his fall. Tommy moved quickly to try and retrieve the fallen container, but almost all the water had spilt onto the grass.

'Sorry,' said Peter.

'Now what will we do?' asked Susie.

'I'll go down to one of the cottages and ask them to fill it,' answered Peter.

'Butter fingers!' said Tommy mockingly.

Peter shrugged as though ruefully accepting the criticism, then he turned in Annie's direction. She was looking at him curiously, and he felt a tiny shiver run up his spine. *Did she suspect he had staged the fall?* No, he told himself, it was probably his imagination. At least he hoped so.

'Here, I'll come with you,' offered Tommy.

'No, that's OK, you look after the fire,' said Peter, quickly lifting his bicycle and starting for the nearby road. 'I won't be long.'

Before Tommy could argue or either of the girls could offer to join him, he was on his way, swiftly guiding his bicycle through a gap in the hedge, then cycling down the hill towards the bridge. He knew this area well and soon reached the turn that led up a short lane to Willow Cottage. He rode to the cottage, then dismounted from the bike, parking it behind a hedge. He moved quickly now, opening the saddle bag and taking out the package that Mr Mc Mahon had given him yesterday to take home in his bait box. It was a soft, bulky envelope – certainly not guns or weapons – and Peter would have loved to know what it contained. He knew better than to peek into it however, and now he held it down by his side and knocked on the cottage door.

Before long the door was opened by a stocky man in his early sixties, with curly grey hair. He was unshaven and wearing a discoloured vest and moleskin trousers, and if he had been expecting Peter's visit, he gave nothing away.

'Yes?' he said.

'I've been told to give you this,' said Peter, indicating the envelope. 'My friends think I've gone to refill my billy-can, so I can't stay long.'

The man glanced around as if to make sure that Peter truly was alone, then he opened the doorway.

'Come in,' he said.

Peter stepped into the cottage, its interior dark after the sunshine outside. He got the smell of a dog, although none was to be seen.

'I'll take that,' said the man, 'You can get your water from the pitcher.'

'Thanks,' replied Peter, going over to the large jug of water on the kitchen table, and starting to fill the billy-can. Out of the corner of his eye he noticed that the man didn't open the package, but slipped it into the drawer of a tall pine dresser.

Peter filled the billy-can, then turned back to the man, remembering his manners.

'By the way, I'm …'

'Don't tell me!' said the man sharply, cutting him short with a raised hand.

Peter was taken aback, and he realised that he must have looked a bit shocked because the man softened his tone now and spoke more sympathetically.

'Better that way, son. I can't give your name, you can't give my name. OK?'

'OK.'

'Good lad. I'll let you be on your way so.'

'Right,' answered Peter. He was tempted to say that if the man was that keen to hide his identity he shouldn't have left a letter on the end of the table, addressed to Mr Ned Morgan. Instead he said, 'Thanks for the water.'

'Sure. Up the Republic!'

'Up the Republic!' answered Peter with a smile, then he nodded farewell and went outside to retrieve his bicycle. Exhilarated at having carried out his mission, he put the sealed billy-can into the saddle bag, mounted up and cycled down the lane and back up the hill to his friends.

As he re-entered the field he saw that Susie and Tommy had the fire going well. He took the billy-can of water from the bike and handed it to Tommy.

'Right, problem solved!' he said cheerfully.

'You're still a butter fingers,' said Tommy with a grin.

'Yeah, and you supposed to be a star rugby player,' said Susie in mock criticism as she raked the fire, clearing a place onto which Tommy could lower the billy-can.

Peter tried for a sheepish grin, then turned round to Annie. Once again he got the impression that she had been observing him, and while she simply gave a small smile he felt a tiny tingle go up his spine again. *No,* he told himself, *she couldn't know what he had been up to.* But somehow, he sensed that she was sharper and more observant than Susie or Tommy, and that he would have to be more careful in future. For now, though, it was important to act as though nothing was amiss, and he looked Annie in the eye and smiled.

'All right,' he said, 'let's have this famous apple tart!'

CHAPTER NINE

Disagreements were strange things, Annie thought, as she walked home from the Irish club with Susie, Tommy and Peter. Her father had always claimed that you couldn't call someone a proper friend until you had a row and managed to get over it. Annie wasn't sure about that, though she understood Da's view that real friendships survived the odd storm. And tonight she had had her first disagreement with her new friend Peter.

It was late June now, and in the weeks that had passed since her first visit to Susie's house her friendship with Susie, Tommy and Peter had blossomed. They had played rounders together, gone on picnics, had races in Nugent's Field, and fished and swam in the river Tolka. There had always been playful arguing and teasing, but never a serious disagreement until tonight.

The four of them had been leaving the club to walk home when the subject of the Wilson assassination had come up. Field Marshall Sir Henry Wilson was a British MP who had been security advisor to the new Northern Ireland government, and earlier in the day he had been shot dead in London by two republican gunmen. Although Annie was aware that Peter held nationalist views, she had still been a bit shocked when he announced that he was pleased at the news.

'He was retired from the army,' she had argued. 'He was just walking home and they shot him dead. How can that be good?'

'He was the enemy, Annie,' answered Peter unapologetically. 'He was dead against Irish freedom.'

'Then why didn't they kill him when he was in the army? When the War of Independence was on?'

'They didn't get a chance then.'

'But now we're getting a Free State and the British are leaving. So what's the point in killing Mr Wilson?'

'The British aren't leaving Northern Ireland. And Wilson was up to his eyes in what's happening there.'

'So it's OK to kill him?'

'He was a soldier all his life. How many people do you think he killed? But nobody calls him a murderer; he just gets medals from the King.'

Annie could see that Peter really believed he was right, and she didn't want to fall out with him. But some things were just wrong and she couldn't pretend otherwise.

'It's not the same, Peter. Not when there's the Treaty.'

'The Treaty?' said Peter derisively.

'It was the best deal Michael Collins could get from the British,' Susie chipped in. 'My dad said so.'

'Well, your dad is wrong, Susie,' replied Peter. 'Unless he fancies swearing allegiance to the King of England. Well, does he?'

'No', said Tommy. 'But still.'

'Still what?'

Susie and Tommy didn't have the confidence or the arguments to challenge Peter and Annie felt annoyed on their behalf.

'For God's sake, Peter!' she interjected. 'What about the election? The people just voted by a mile for the new government and the Treaty!'

'Mr de Valera says the majority haven't the right to be wrong.'

Eamon de Valera, the leader of the anti-Treaty forces, was held in respect by many people, but Annie felt that this was still a smart-aleck answer.

'So he decides if the people are right or wrong?' she said. 'Sure in that case you might as well not *have* elections at all.'

She looked at Peter and could see that he was struggling to answer this.

'I don't care what you say, Annie,' he said finally. 'I'm not sorry they killed Wilson.'

'And I don't care what you say; it still sounds like murder to me.'

There was a moment's awkwardness, then Susie broke the silence. 'Well, *we* can't do anything about any of it. So we might as well get on, and all be friends. Amn't I right?' she said in an encouraging tone as she looked Annie in the eye.

'Yeah, you are,' answered Annie, pleased that Susie was offering a way out of the argument.

Susie turned to Peter. 'Amn't I right, Peter?'

Peter hesitated, and Annie hoped he wasn't going to continue to argue. Then he gave a wry smile and nodded to Susie. 'Yeah, you're right.'

'Good,' she answered. 'So, to cheer us all up, why did the cook get arrested?'

'What?' asked Tommy.

'Why did the cook get arrested?' repeated Susie.

'Why?'

'Because he beat up an egg!'

'That's the worst joke I ever heard,' protested Tommy, but even as he said it he was smiling, and Annie and Peter laughed with Susie, the earlier tension eased.

They made their way up Dorset Street towards Drumcondra, chatting about their plans for the summer and the new popular song 'I'm Just Wild About Harry', that Susie was learning on the piano. Clanking trams ran along the busy thoroughfare, but they were happy to walk, strolling along at an easy pace. Annie was glad that the argument hadn't been allowed to fester, especially as the Scanlons were about to go on holidays and she wouldn't see Peter for several weeks. At the same time, she wasn't sure if things were really all right between herself and Peter or if everyone was just being polite.

There had been talk earlier in the week of having a farewell gathering for all of them in the Scanlon's house on Sunday, before his family went away. Now, as they turned into St Alphonsus Avenue, Annie wondered if this would still happen, or if Peter might decide to be a bit cool because of the argument. She found herself feeling surprisingly anxious as they approached her house.

'Well,' she said, stopping at her hall door, 'I'll see you all…'

'Of course,' said Susie.

'Yeah, 'night, Annie,' said Tommy.

Peter looked her in the eye, then said casually. 'Will we see you on Sunday? About three o'clock?'

'Great,' said Annie equally casually. 'See you then.'

Everyone exchanged waves, and the others set off. Annie breathed a small sigh of relief, then she smiled, opened the door and happily entered the house.

* * *

Peter stopped dead in his tracks. He had been walking up the laneway from his house to Botanic Road with the intention of calling
for Tommy when he recognised the figure sitting on the bench at
the corner of the main road, a newspaper casually held out before
him. It was the gunman he had rescued from the Black and Tans
and who had spoken to Mr McMahon at the Irish language club.

Peter knew at once that the man's presence wasn't an accident,
and his first thought was that perhaps something had happened
to Mc Mahon and the other man was here to tip him off. In that
case, stopping dead hadn't been the cleverest of responses and he
immediately resumed walking, keeping his stride as casual as possible. He drew level with the man, who rose from the seat and
folded his newspaper.

'Morning, Peter,' he said. 'Walk along with me for a minute,
nice and relaxed like.'

Peter nodded in agreement. 'Right.'

'You weren't headed anywhere urgent, were you?'

'Just going to call for my friend Tommy.'

'You can see him later.'

'I suppose. Is everything OK with Mr Mac?'

'Sure. But he couldn't make it today. Step into the Botanics
with me, as though we're having a ramble.'

'OK,' answered Peter. The gardens would provide good cover,
with plenty of Saturday morning visitors entering and leaving by
the nearby main entrance.

'Just in case anyone asks, you know me from the Irish club.'

'All right,' said Peter. 'What am I supposed to call you?'

'You don't have to call me anything,' said the man.

Peter felt a stab of irritation. This man knew his name, knew his address, even felt free to wait for him coming out of his house, yet Peter knew nothing, absolutely nothing, about him.

'If you can know all about me, why can't I at least call you something? Even your first name?'

The man gave a crooked grin. 'Feisty, aren't you? All right, it's Finbar. No need to get into surnames, OK?'

'OK.'

They reached the main entrance to the Botanical Gardens and stepped in through the wrought iron gates. Finbar indicated a pathway that led away from the tall glasshouses, towards which a lot of the visitors were making. They followed the path, then took a turn that brought them to a quieter section of the gardens.

'All right, we won't be heard here,' said Finbar as they strolled along. 'First of all, well done on the messages so far. Mr Mac is impressed with you.'

'Really?' said Peter, unable to hide his pleasure.

'Oh yes. But I'm not surprised. I knew from that day in North Earl Street that you're cool in a tight corner.'

'Thanks, Finbar.'

'I'm only telling the truth. But things are changing now – coming to a head.'

'How do you mean?'

'Our lads in the Four Courts have really made their presence felt. Between that and Wilson being shot, the English are hopping mad.'

'Pity about them,' said Peter, his views on the shooting unchanged despite Annie's arguments of a couple of nights previously.

'Absolutely. But they're putting huge pressure on the new government to come down hard on us. So far, Collins hasn't attacked the Four Courts, but the heat is coming on.'

'Right.'

'So that means some of our safe houses aren't going to be so safe in future,' said Finbar. 'Like the one you know – Willow Cottage.'

'OK.'

'We have to get stuff out of there in case it's raided. And we need somewhere secure to store certain items. Mr Mac said your house has big gardens. Any chance you could hide some stuff?'

Peter hadn't been expecting this and he hesitated.

'If you can't, say so. Nobody will think the worse of you.'

'No, it's not that,' said Peter, his excitement mounting. 'I *can* hide things for you, but I've a better place than our garden.'

'Where?'

'Here. You can get from our garden into the Bots, and there're loads of places here where stuff would never be found.'

'Are you sure?' 'Certain. I've played hide and seek here since I was small. I know it inside out. It would be way safer than our garden – but I can still get my hands on the stuff in a couple of minutes.'

Finbar looked thoughtful, then nodded. 'That might work out well.'

'When do you want to do this?' asked Peter.

'As soon as possible. Today or tomorrow. We heard that the cottage could be raided early next week.'

'OK.'

'Find some excuse to cycle back there over the weekend. If the curtains are open everything is fine. If the curtains are drawn just cycle past and don't stop.'

'Right.'

'Then hide what you're given till you hear from us. And thanks, Peter. This won't be forgotten.'

'You're grand.'

'One last thing. What's your phone number at home?'

'Eh … 4827. But my mother often answers the phone.'

'Don't worry, we'd only ever phone if it was urgent.'

'All right.'

'OK, that's everything. Any questions?'

Peter had countless questions, but he knew that Finbar probably wouldn't answer most of them. When he didn't immediately voice any queries, Finbar nodded, as though satisfied at Peter's discretion.

'Good man. We'll be in touch. Up the Republic.'

'Up the Republic,' responded Peter, but already Finbar was moving away. Peter hesitated a moment, slightly thrown by the gunman's abrupt departure. Then he continued walking, a little scared at what he had taken on, but excited too, and eager for his new, more active role.

CHAPTER TEN

▬ ▬ ▬

Annie hadn't planned to eavesdrop. But she couldn't help it if her parents had left the kitchen door open, could she? And besides, it was her they were talking about, so it wasn't as if she was ear-wigging on someone else's business.

It was Sunday morning and earlier the family had dressed up for Mass, then come back for the fry-up breakfast that Da sometimes did on Sunday before he went for a pint in the Cat and Cage pub. Annie was sitting on the end of her bed, the sunlight warm upon her favourite pink candlewick bedspread. The bedroom door was slightly ajar and she had the children's page of Da's newspaper open before her. She was wearing her best dress, a dark green velvet one with white lace that Ma had bought her last Christmas, and that Annie felt would look nice and smart for the farewell gathering in Peter's house later today. Now, though, she listened as her parents argued about her summer job.

'I should have been consulted,' said Da.

'Mick thought he was doing Annie a good turn,' argued Ma.

'I'm sure he meant well, but I still should have been consulted.'

Maybe I could have been consulted, Annie felt like shouting down to them.

Mick was Ma's eldest brother, and he had dropped in briefly

while Da was at the pub. Although her mother hadn't called Annie down to tell her, it seemed that Mick had organised a job for her. She had finished primary school the previous Friday, and even though she was looking forward to starting in Eccles Street, she had still felt a little tearful saying her last goodbyes to her class-mates in St Mary's. But there wasn't time to be sentimental for long, and the sooner she got a summer job, the sooner she could bring in some money to go towards the cost of sending her to Eccles Street.

'Don't always throw Mick's goodness in his face,' said Ma now, in a rare show of irritation with her husband.

'I don't, Maura,' said Da, making his tone more reasonable. 'I just think he could have mentioned it to me before setting every-thing up.'

Annie knew that Da didn't particularly like her Uncle Mick. She suspected that it was partly because of Mick's cocky manner, but mostly to do with Da's pride. Mick had been active in the War of Independence and now he had contacts among those who had taken power. It was through Mick that Da had got the job of transporting senior officials and ministers in the new government, and while Da was glad to have the work, it bothered him to be under a compliment to his brother-in law.

'Well he told *me* to tell you, so what's the difference?' said Ma.

Annie rose from the bed and made for the stairs. She was tired of listening to her parents arguing about who should have been told about this job – she herself had been told nothing! She came down the stairs and entered the kitchen.

'Ah, Annie,' her father said pleasantly, giving no indication that he had been arguing. 'The very girl.'

Annie couldn't admit to listening to their conversation, so she looked at him innocently. 'Yes, Da?'

'Your ma and I have good news for you.'

'Great. What is it?'

'Your uncle Mick has got you a little job,' said her mother, and Annie had to suppress a smile at the way Ma had reclaimed the credit for her brother. 'You'll be starting tomorrow.'

'Grand,' said Annie. She wouldn't have minded a few days off between the end of school and the summer job, but she wasn't going to complain. 'Where will I be working?'

'In town,' said Da. 'Only about a fifteen minute walk away.'

'It's in a shop, our Mick knows the owner.'

'Brilliant,' said Annie. 'What kind of shop?'

'A fishmongers,' answered Ma. 'Just off Henry Street.'

A fishmongers!? Annie didn't like the smell of fish and she hated their dead-eyed look as the lay on the slab of the local fishmongers. But the money was needed and she didn't want to disappoint her parents. 'Great,' she said. 'Tell Uncle Mick – tell him thanks a million.'

* * *

Peter was feeling pleased with himself. Yesterday he had successfully transferred a small, sealed sack from the cottage at Cardiffs Bridge to his back garden. From there he had safely moved it to his favourite hiding place under an old slab in a rarely visited corner of the maintenance section of the Botanical Gardens. And now he was in the kitchen, loading a tray to bring bowls of strawberries and cream to his friends in the back garden. All in all, it was turning out to be a good weekend. The one downside was that his family was going on their annual holiday to Carlingford later in the week, and so he wouldn't be available to do any missions for Mr Mac or Finbar. With tension rising between the pro- and anti-Treaty forces there was every chance of fighting breaking out, but he had to go away, and Mr Mac understood that, so there was no point worrying about what he might miss.

Peter placed a spoon in each bowl, then covered the strawberries with a generous dollop of cream, resisting the temptation to taste his own portion before joining his friends. He was glad that he had suggested a farewell gathering, especially considering his argument with Annie on Thursday night. He didn't want to fall out with her, and he was glad that there had seemed to be no lingering coolness when she had shown up today. He was just about to lift the tray when his mother entered the kitchen.

'Strawberries and cream – the taste of summer!' she said.

'Yeah, it's brilliant the way they go together,' answered Peter.

'It will be a nice treat for your little friend.'

Peter felt a dart of irritation. He hated the way his mother referred to Annie as 'his little friend'. She didn't call Tommy or Susie his little friends. 'It will be a nice treat for *all* my friends,' he replied.

'Well, yes, of course,' answered his mother, as though that was what she had meant all along.

It wasn't, though, and Peter knew it. His mother had been unfailingly polite whenever she met Annie, but she could never quite disguise the fact that she was being agreeable to someone she regarded as lower in rank to his other friends. So Annie's family wasn't as well-off as his, but why should that matter?

'Excuse me,' he said, nodding slightly curtly to his mother and lifting the tray. He stepped out the back door of the kitchen and into the garden, then crossed the lawn towards where his friends were sitting in deck chairs under the shade of a tall sycamore tree.

'Get a move on, slave!' cried Susie, 'We're tired waiting!'

'How would you like it all over you?' asked Peter.

Susie put her head to one side as though considering. 'Eh, no thanks, I'd prefer to eat it!'

Peter laid down the tray, indicating for them all to help themselves.

'This is lovely, Peter' said Annie, smiling enthusiastically as she ate hers.

'It is, isn't it?' He smiled back, realising how much he liked her. He was really glad that they hadn't parted for the summer break on an argument.

Tommy nodded approvingly. 'I love the way the cream and the strawberries sort of mush in together in your mouth.'

'You've such a way with words, Tommy!' said Susie.

'Well they do,' insisted Tommy, 'it's a great taste.'

'Well done, Peter, for thinking up a farewell party,' said Susie. 'Though I wish we weren't all going to be split up.'

'Me too,' said Annie. 'Where will your family be going, Susie?'

'Same place as always.' She turned to her twin brother and together they chanted mockingly, 'Wexford, where the strawberries grow!'

'But isn't Wexford really nice?' asked Annie.

'It's grand,' said Susie. 'It's just that we always go to the exact same place in Rosslare Strand. And I'll miss seeing you – and even this galoot here!'

'Thanks for that, Susie,' said Peter sarcastically.

'We should write to each other,' said Susie. 'If we send each other postcards it won't really seem like the gang's broken up. What do you think?'

Peter nodded. 'Yeah, why not?'

'I'd love to get cards all right,' said Annie. 'But I don't know about sending them. They hardly sell postcards of Hickey's Fishmongers!'

'Just send us a postcard of Dublin then,' said Susie.

'Fair enough,' agreed Annie, then she grinned. 'Here, talking of post, what do you get if you cross an elephant with a vicious dog?'

'What?' asked Tommy.

'A nervous postman!'

The others laughed, then Peter indicated the lemonade glasses that they had put aside when eating the strawberries and cream. 'We should have a toast,' he said. 'We're going to be split up, but here's to when we all get back together.' Careful not to spill the lemonade, he raised his glass, and the others did the same. They clinked glasses, giggling, then Susie raised her hand for attention.

'And as Daddy always says on New Year's Eve,' and here she mimicked her father's deep, serious voice. '*Here's to the future, and all the good it holds!*'

They raised their glasses again, and Peter wondered what the future *did* hold. The thought struck him that it could be bad as well as good. Then he saw his friends' smiling faces, and he dismissed the thought, and eagerly joined the toast.

PART TWO

———

CIVIL WAR

CHAPTER ELEVEN

— — — —

Annie had the cleanest hands in Dublin. At least that's what Mr Hickey, the fishmonger, laughingly claimed whenever he saw her washing them vigorously with carbolic soap. But Annie was determined that she wouldn't smell of fish when she took her lunch break or when she finished work in the evenings. Today, Wednesday, was her third day in Hickeys and she had been pleasantly surprised at how much she enjoyed the work. OK, there was a strong smell of fish in the shop, but she was used to it now and she was no longer put off by the rows of fish with bulging eyes that stared lifelessly across the ice-filled marble slab. There was always good-humoured banter, too, between Mr Hickey and the customers, particularly with the sharp-tongued men who delivered supplies from the fish markets.

Mrs Hickey, the wife of the owner, was a bit cranky, and Annie hated the way she was really polite to well-heeled customers, but just business-like to people who were obviously poorer. Mr Hickey made up for it, though, and Annie liked working with him. The hours were long, and when the shop was busy Annie was run ragged serving and packing the fish, but both evenings when they finished, Mr Hickey had slipped her a couple of fresh fish to take home. When Annie had looked surprised, Mr Hickey had winked and said: 'Perk of the job – just don't tell the missus!'

Annie had agreed, happy to outsmart the stern-faced Mrs Hickey. And even though she hadn't received her first week's wages yet, Annie had felt like a real worker when she arrived home and presented Ma with the fish her boss had given her.

'Good girl, Annie,' Ma had said. 'They must be pleased with you. Uncle Mick will be delighted.'

Annie had been glad to see Ma happy, and although one part of her envied her friends and their trips to Carlingford and Wexford, she had been glad of the chance to give something back to the family.

Now she was out shopping with Ma, and it made her feel grown up to think that she would be contributing also to the new clothes that were being bought for when she started in Eccles Street. She had arranged to meet Ma during her break, and had run happily from Henry Street to Capel Street, where they wanted to look at reasonably priced new shoes for school.

'What about these ones, Annie?' asked Ma, showing her a sensible pair of heavy black shoes.

'They're a bit …'

'What?'

'I know we want something that will last, Ma, but … well, they look like clodhoppers.'

Ma laughed. 'Aren't you the devil for style. Maybe it's a pair of fancy lady's ankle boots you want?'

Annie looked appealingly at her mother. 'Maybe something in between?'

'Oh, all right then.'

Ma was about to comment further when both of them were shocked by a thunderous noise.

'Jesus, Mary and Joseph!' cried Ma.

'What was that?!' said Annie, her heart thumping with fright.

'Artillery,' answered a man who had been trying on shoes in the aisle beside them.

There was another loud bang, and Annie jumped again.

'Eighteen pounders,' said the man. 'I'd know that sound anywhere.'

It was a horrible sound and Annie braced herself in case there was another explosion.

'Where's it coming from?' asked Ma.

'Has to be the Four Courts,' answered the man.

The Four Courts complex was only a couple of hundred yards away – no wonder the sound had been so frightening, Annie thought. But although the courts had been occupied by republican rebels for weeks now, so far there had been no fighting. 'What do you think is happening, Ma?' she asked.

'I don't know, pet. Maybe the government is taking the place back.'

'Can't be anything else,' said the man. 'The rebels have no artillery.'

There was another loud bang, but this time Annie forced herself not to jump.

Ma shook her head sadly. 'There's going to be people killed. This is madness.'

'It's more than that, missus,' said the man solemnly. 'It's war. There's no going back now.'

Annie didn't know how that would affect her family, but she felt a stab of anxiety. And she sensed, somehow, that it *was* going to affect them.

✷ ✷ ✷

Peter cycled at speed down Phibsboro Road, eager to get to the heart of the action. Even from here, almost a mile from the embattled Four Courts, he could see black smoke rising against the blue of the summer sky. It was two days now since the new government had launched its assault on the rebels, and somehow, against all the odds, the republicans were still holding out.

Peter's family had had their holiday plans disrupted due to heavy fighting in the city between the rebels and the army. Sackville Street was now a battle zone, and so the family had cancelled their plan to get the train at Amiens Street station for the journey to Carlingford. Instead, they were going to avoid the centre of town altogether and board the train north of the city at Killester – assuming the trains were still running tonight. Peter fervently hoped that they wouldn't be. How frustrating it would feel to be out of circulation while a decisive battle was being fought in Dublin.

When the first shots were fired two days ago he had cycled to the cottage at Cardiffs Bridge, to offer his services to the rebels, but there had been nobody there. He had left a note volunteering to help in any way he could, but there had been no phone call from either Mr McMahon or Finbar, and Peter had felt frustratingly sidelined as the battle raged between the army and the rebels.

It was an unequal contest, with the new national army possessing armoured cars, artillery and even aeroplanes that they had acquired from the British government. Peter believed, though, that the rebels had right on their side and total conviction – factors that eventually brought victory in the War of Independence, which had also been fought against a bigger and far better-equipped army.

He reached the bottom of Phibsboro Road, and as he swung round the curve onto Constitution Hill, he had a vista of the city below him. From here he could see that the Four Courts were ablaze, and in the distance he could hear the rattle of machine gun and rifle fire. His parents would be horrified if they knew he was here, but he had told his mother that he was cycling to Drumcondra to visit a classmate from Belvedere. It was a bare-faced lie, but he had to get to where the action was.

He wasn't sure what he would do when he got there, but he cycled rapidly down Constitution Hill, the sound of shooting becoming louder as he neared Church Street. People were out on the pavements, watching the flames and plumes of smoke that bellowed dramatically from the Four Courts. Peter cycled on, rising in the saddle as his bicycle bounced over the cobbled surface of the road. He reached the junction of King Street, then slowed, seeing the road ahead blocked off by two armoured cars and a cordon of troops.

Peter dismounted and approached a man wearing an officer's uniform.

'What's happening in the Four Courts, sir?' he asked politely. He knew from experience that a boy who was well spoken and courteous could ask questions like this and have a good chance of getting a proper answer.

The officer looked at him briefly, then replied. 'It's all over bar the shouting,' he said, a hint of boastfulness in his tone.

'Really?'

'We've taken the building. A few diehards are fighting a retreat, but the rest have all been killed or captured.

'Right,' said Peter, trying not to show his disappointment.

'It was only a matter of time,' continued the officer. 'They were just too thick to know when they were beaten.'

Peter felt offended. How could this man not recognise the bravery of the rebels who had fought for two days despite being heavily outnumbered and bombarded with artillery? But before he could think up an answer there was the most shattering explosion that Peter had ever heard.

Everyone started in fright, and nearby window panes shattered. Peter instinctively put up his hands to protect his face, then, realising that he hadn't been hit by flying glass, he lowered them and saw an amazing sight. A vast plume of smoke had shot into the sky above the Four Courts. It rose hundreds of feet, like pictures that Peter had seen of erupting volcanoes, and he watched, mesmerised.

'Must have been their ammo stores,' one of the soldiers said.

'Must have,' said the officer who had been so boastful a moment ago.

If the ammunition had gone up there could be further explosions. It was time to get out of here, Peter decided. He picked up his bicycle, then turned back to the officer.

'All over bar the shouting? I don't think so, mister!' he said. Then, before the man could react, Peter jumped up on the bicycle and rode quickly away.

* * *

Annie made her way carefully past burnt-out shops, avoiding the debris that cluttered the city pavements after a week of fierce fighting. The Four Courts complex was now a charred shell, and enormous damage had been done to parts of the city's main thoroughfare, Sackville Street.

Annie crossed its broad expanse as she made her way to work in Henry Street. It was her first day back, since the fishmongers had had to close due to the battles in the centre of town. The city had finally been made secure by the government troops, but there had been many soldiers killed and wounded on both sides before the rebels had been driven from Dublin. There had also been hundreds of civilian casualties from heavy fighting near areas that were densely populated.

Annie had overheard these details from Uncle Mick, who had bitterly criticised the rebels, and said that the government troops would vigorously go on the offensive to take control of the many areas outside Dublin that were still under rebel control.

Mick had been really angry, and Annie had also overheard him telling Ma that the rebels had seriously underestimated Michael Collins. But, regardless of who had done what, or why, Annie thought it was a tragedy to see so much death and destruction. She made her way around a party of workmen who were clearing debris from outside the ruined shops where beautiful clothes had been destroyed, and undoubtedly, people's livelihoods had been put at risk. The fighting had cost her a week's wages, but she had no right to feel sorry for herself, not when other people had lost everything.

During her week of enforced idleness she had tried not to dwell on the bad news and to get on with things as normal. She had played with her friends on the road, often against a backdrop of cannon and small arms fire from the city centre. With Susie, Tommy and Peter all gone away with their families, she missed the fun she had become used to with her new group of friends. The other girls on the road hadn't shunned her – she had never stopped playing with them, even when getting friendlier with her new group – but there was a slight distance between them now, a distance that Josie Gogarty had been subtly doing her best to reinforce.

Annie had ignored the other girl's sly jibes, and, being the fastest girl on the road, she usually still got picked first for chasing games, but even so, there was a change with her old friends that was a bit unsettling. And now, despite her initial misgivings about working in a fishmongers, Annie was actually looking forward to work as she turned into Henry Street. She didn't like the smell of porter that came from the pub at the corner, so she crossed the road, then made her way along the opposite side until she reached the fish shop.

'If it's not the bould Annie!' said Mr Hickey. 'Welcome back.'

'Thanks, Mr Hickey,' said Annie with a smile. 'Good morning, Mrs Hickey'

The fishmonger's wife nodded briefly in greeting, then looked at Annie, her gaze more stern than usual. 'You need to get your apron on at once and start serving – we've lost a full week's takings,' she said.

Annie felt a flash of anger. Mrs Hickey had spoken as though Annie were in some way responsible for the lost earnings. And as for starting at once, it wasn't as though Annie was late – in fact she was several minutes early. She was grateful that Uncle

Mick's friendship with Mr Hickey had got her this job, but it shouldn't mean that she had to accept being bullied. It was completely unfair of Mrs Hickey to take it out on her over the lost earnings, and Annie felt butterflies in her tummy, but she looked the woman in the eye.

'I'm sorry you lost a week's takings,' she said, keeping her tone polite. 'But other people lost their jobs, and their homes, even their lives.'

Mrs Hickey looked completely taken aback, and before she could think up a response, Annie quickly finished the conversation.

'I'll get my apron now and start serving.' She nodded to Mrs Hickey, turned on her heel and walked swiftly into the back of the shop.

CHAPTER TWELVE

▬   ▬   ▬   ▬

Peter tried not to let his frustration show as he walked along the fairway of the golf course. It was a glorious late July day, and he was caddying for his father who had come to Carlingford for the last two weeks of the family's month-long holiday. His father was playing another dentist, Mr Boyd, a thin, angular man with a Northern accent that Peter sometimes found difficult to understand. Mr Boyd had hired a professional caddy, a small, deeply-tanned man who spoke as little as possible, and so Peter was left to his own thoughts as they all followed the beautifully manicured fairways of the golf course.

He could see the mountains of Mourne ahead, dramatically silhouetted against the blue sky as they swept down to the sea, just like in the famous song that his sister Mary sometimes sang at parties. But in contrast to the picturesque setting, Peter's mood was dark.

His father and Mr Boyd were discussing the civil war, and the news wasn't good. Despite their defeat in Dublin, the rebels had originally held much of the territory outside the capital, but the national army had been greatly expanded, and now they were driving the rebels from one town after another. The cities of Limerick and Waterford had just been retaken by the government forces, and Mr Boyd was enthusiastic about their progress.

'A damn good thrashing is what the rebels are getting,' he said. 'Only a matter of time till the army mops them up.'

'I hope so,' said Peter's father. 'They still hold Cork city, though, and they're strong in the southwest.'

'But they're a raggle-taggle lot, Henry. Gunmen who are half-gangster, half-fanatic.'

Peter thought this was a terrible slur on brave men, though he could hardly tackle an adult, especially about a conversation on which he was eavesdropping. But who was Mr Boyd, or even his father, to make judgements on people who were risking their lives – while they themselves played golf? If Mr Boyd felt all that strongly, why wasn't he out fighting on the pro-Treaty side?

Peter had tried unsuccessfully to contact Mr Mac or Finbar before leaving for Carlingford, and although he enjoyed the fun of meeting up with his cousins and extended family during the holiday in county Louth, he still felt frustrated – and even slightly guilty – to be away from the action at this crucial time.

The golf party stopped now where the two players' balls lay in line with each other. The wizened caddy withdrew a club without a word and handed it to Mr Boyd.

'Six iron, please, Peter,' said his father, and Peter took the club from the golf bag.

Both men hit well. Mr Boyd's was a particularly long, straight shot, and he looked pleased with himself as the party moved off again, the caddy wordlessly leading the way.

'So, young man,' said Mr Boyd, turning to Peter. 'I'm told you're rather a precise place kicker for Belvedere.'

'Sometimes,' answered Peter. Normally he would be flattered

to have his rugby skills praised by an adult, but something in him rebelled at taking pleasure from Mr Boyd's praise.

'Precision is everything,' said Mr Boyd. 'And of course a key skill for a dentist. I'm sure one day you'll be a great one, like your father.'

Peter didn't want to sound cheeky so he kept his reply reasonable sounding. 'I don't think so,' he answered as they walked along the fairway.

'Come come, no false modesty now,' said Mr Boyd heartily.

'It's not false modesty,' said Peter quietly, even though part of him wanted to shout – *why do you just assume I'm going to be the same as my father?!*

'Then don't underestimate yourself,' answered Mr Boyd, playfully tossing Peter's hair. 'You'll make a fine dentist. Might even give you a run for your money, Henry,' he said, turning with a conspiratorial smile to Peter's father.

Peter knew that he should probably say nothing, but Boyd's behaviour had annoyed him.

'I've no plans to be any kind of a dentist,' he said. He noticed with satisfaction that his father's friend was shocked. His father, too, looked taken aback. Peter's future had never actually been discussed at home, and certainly nobody had asked him his wishes, but an assumption had definitely been made about his career, and this was the first time his father had heard anything to the contrary.

There was an awkward silence for a second or two, and on reaching the spot where his father's ball had landed, Peter saw a chance to change tack. He quickly lowered the bag of golf clubs and withdrew a club. 'I think a nine iron, Dad,' he said.

His father didn't respond at once, and Peter wondered if he was going to get away with changing the subject. His father seemed to weigh up what he was going to do, then he nodded. 'Yes,' he answered. 'I think a nine iron is about right.'

Inwardly, Peter breathed a sigh of relief. This wouldn't be the end of it, of course, and there was sure to be a discussion about family tradition and Peter's future – not to mention a reprimand for his behaviour this morning. But for now he had managed to silence Mr Boyd, and that was really satisfying. He handed his father the club, then stood back and watched his shot soar up into the blue summer sky, feeling better than he had all morning.

✱ ✱ ✱

Annie knew that her mother wouldn't open a letter addressed to her, but postcards were different, and Ma would have read any cards that arrived while Annie was in work. It was just as well that Peter's card from Carlingford had no personal things in it, and had just described how he was having fun swimming and fishing during his family holiday. Anything more intimate and Annie was sure she would have been teased by her parents and her brothers about having a boyfriend. It was an embarrassing thing that adults did, and Annie could never see what was supposed to be funny about it. Even as it was, Eamon and Sean had tried to goad her about the postcard, but she had told them not to be stupid.

Now she sat down to read the latest card from Susie, as Ma fried some fresh plaice that Mr Hickey had given her after work. She had settled in well at the shop, and after four weeks there she had completely overcome her distaste for the staring eyes of dead fish.

She still washed her hands vigorously after work, though, to be certain they didn't smell, much to the amusement of Mr Hickey. She had made an extra effort to get on with his wife, who seemed to have grudgingly accepted that Annie was a good worker, so that Mr Hickey no longer had to hide it when he gave Annie free portions of fish.

Today's offering was sizzling appetisingly in the pan as she sat down with Susie's postcard. The card was a photograph of the sea at Wexford, and Annie turned it over and read Susie's deliberately small writing that packed every available piece of space.

Dear Annie,

Greetings from Wexford where the sea is so cold my skin turned blue! Tommy laughed at my goosebumps, but I laughed at him when we crossed a field and he stepped in a cowpat! We went to a circus, but the clowns weren't funny. The acrobats were great, my heart was in my mouth. Going now for ice-cream, yum, yum, yum! See you soon, your friend, Susie.

ps. only six weeks till we enter Ecland!

Susie had begun calling Eccles Street 'Ecland,' and Annie smiled now at her friend's colourful wording and breathless writing style. She was enjoying Susie's enthusiasm, even on a second reading, when she heard the hall door being closed, and her father came into the kitchen. He greeted Ma, then turned to Annie. She thought he looked tired, but he smiled at her.

'How's my girl?'

'Fine thanks, Da.'

'Fish for dinner, what?'

'Yeah, I told Mr Hickey you loved the last bit of plaice.'

'I hope you didn't make us out to be a charity case, love,' her father said.

'It wasn't like that, Da. I just said you loved it.'

'Right,' said Da, a little uncertainly.

Annie knew that her father believed in providing for his family and didn't like being under a compliment to anyone. Several times she had heard her brothers talking about the 1913 lockout, and she reckoned that Da's attitude stemmed from that troubled time. Annie was too young to remember so far back, but it seemed that Da had been a member of Jim Larkin's union, and when Larkin had clashed with the employers of Dublin, thousands of workers had been locked out of their jobs and had gone hungry. She had heard Da saying that the anti-Treaty rebels could have learned from the union leader's tactics of fighting hard, but recognising when you had the best deal you were going to get.

Despite his respect for Larkin, it was after the lockout that Da had branched out for himself, working hard as a hackney driver. Annie guessed that he never again wanted to depend on wages that an employer could withhold. It made sense of why he had gone into debt to buy the Model T, and why he worked long, irregular hours. It made sense, too, of why he accepted work that came through Uncle Mick, despite his reservations about his brother-in-law. Annie admired him for it, but her thoughts were interrupted as her mother turned to Da.

'How did you get on today?' she asked.

'Busy.'

'Thank God for Mick's connections.'

Her mother said it lightly, but Annie suspected that she was playfully ribbing Da.

'Yeah,' he answered evenly, not rising to the bait.

'Where were you working?' asked Ma.

'Would you believe, I'm not supposed to say?'

Annie's ears pricked up at this. 'Why is it a secret, Da?'

'I was driving government people, so they're nervous about anyone knowing their movements.'

Her mother's earlier ribbing tone was gone completely now. 'Is this risky, Jim?' she asked.

'I wouldn't say so,' her husband replied. 'But the rebels have a lot of sympathisers, so some of the government people are anxious that no-one reports their movements – just in case.'

'Just in case what, Da?' asked Annie. 'Could the rebels attack you?'

'Sure why would they, I'm just a fella doing his job. And the government people are probably over-reacting – the rebels aren't strong in Dublin any more.'

'No?' queried Annie.

'No, they were well beaten here in the city. Don't worry, I'll be fine.'

Just then Ma put the fish onto three plates, with a big helping of chips and vegetables that she had already prepared. They all sat down and Da spoke cheerily. 'So, fish and chips – and the fish costing nothing! What more could we ask for?'

He smiled at Annie, and she smiled back, then Ma said grace and they all began eating.

Annie wasn't convinced by her father's answers, however, and she worried that maybe he was doing dangerous driving jobs to earn money for her education. She didn't voice her fears. Instead she ate the tasty plaice, but though she had really been looking forward to her fish and chips, the edge had suddenly gone off her appetite.

■ ■ ■ ■ ■

CHAPTER THIRTEEN

'OK,' said Susie, 'I have the best riddle ever!'

Peter, Tommy and Annie groaned in mock protest, even though Susie's riddles were usually entertaining. It was the first time that the four friends had gathered since they had come back from holidays, and the others were in good spirits as they sat in their usual spot under the sycamore tree at the end of Peter's garden.

'Give me a sentence with the words *defence*, *defeat* and *detail* in it,' said Susie.

'That's not really a riddle,' objected Peter.

'God, you'd argue with your toe-nails!' declared Susie.

'Well it's more a question than a riddle.'

'Sure what's a riddle, except a question that's fun?'

Before Peter could think up a reply to that, Annie spoke.

'OK, I've an answer. What about: "Because of their poor *defence*, the football team suffered a *defeat*, which the newspaper described in *detail*."'

Susie sighed in playful exasperation. 'Do you know what your trouble is, Annie? You're too bright!'

'I think that's a pretty good answer,' said Tommy.

Susie turned to her twin brother. 'Of course it's a good answer. Why do you think she won a scholarship?'

Peter could see that Annie was uncomfortable with Susie singing her praises, and so he spoke up. 'Well, what's the right answer?'

Susie adopted a completely straight face, then slowly replied. 'When the horse jumps over *de fence, de feet* go before *de tail*!'

Tommy groaned, as he generally did at his sister's gags, but Annie laughed and Peter joined in. He was glad that all the gang were back together, he had missed the others while away in Carlingford.

'No contest, Susie,' said Annie, 'your answer wins!'

She smiled as she said it, and Peter noted how she always played down the fact that she was cleverer than most other people. And even though her family wasn't well off, Annie was generous, and today she had given them all bags of jelly sweets that she had bought on a family day trip to the seaside resort of Bray. It had made his mother's reaction all the more annoying earlier on, when Annie had arrived at the house and presented her with a gift of fresh fish from the shop where she worked. His mother had thanked her politely, then Annie had gone out to join Susie and Tommy in the garden, while Peter finished organising glasses of lemonade.

'What an odd thing to do,' his mother had said.

'What's odd about it?'

'Bringing someone a gift of *fish*? It's hardly the done thing.'

'She works in a fish shop, Mum.'

'Quite.'

'How do you mean?'

'Can you imagine me letting Mary or Ann work in a fishmongers?'

'It's just a summer job.'

'And then thinking that I'd appreciate *left-over food*?'

'She was trying to be nice.'

'I'm sure she was. But really, Peter, that's simply not done.'

His mother didn't bother to keep the disdain from her voice, and something in Peter snapped.

'You just have it in for her!' he said.

'No, dear, but–'

'You do, Mum. But she's Susie's friend and now she's my friend too, and I'm not going to have anyone looking down on her!' Peter left immediately with the tray of lemonade-filled glasses, not wanting to get into a full-blown row with his mother.

He felt really irritated with her. She had stopped a week's pocket money as a punishment for his retort to Mr Boyd on the golf course, and now she was insulting his friend. If he was honest though, his mood wasn't helped by the way the war was going. The new national army, equipped with artillery, armour, aeroplanes and ships, was pushing the rebels back all the time. Just a few days earlier the rebels had failed disastrously in a bid to occupy strategically important bridges around Dublin, and large numbers of prisoners had been taken. Most worryingly of all, the government had outmanoeuvred their anti-Treaty opponents by transporting thousands of troops by sea. This surprise move allowed them to bypass the strongholds in the south where the rebels were entrenched, and to attack them from the rear.

Of course the rebels could still engage in widespread guerrilla warfare, and Peter himself was still impatiently waiting for word from either Finbar or Mr Mac. Surely at a time like this they would have wanted the supplies from the hidden sack, he thought, but neither man had rung him, and nobody had responded to the note that he had left at Willow Cottage.

But there was nothing that he could do about any of these things today, and so he deliberately put his worries from his mind and relaxed instead with his friends.

'That was great lemonade,' said Susie as she drained her glass. 'But do you know what's not so great?'

'Your riddles!' said Tommy.

'Don't mind him, Susie,' said Annie.

'I don't.'

'So, what's not great?' asked Peter.

Susie grimaced. 'This time next month you'll be in Belvo, and we'll be starting in Ecland.'

'Why do you have to take the good out of the day by reminding us?' said Tommy. 'I hate when people do that.'

'I'm just saying,' said Susie.

'Anyway, it might be good in Eccles Street,' suggested Annie.

'Or they might be dead strict. That Sister Immaculata looked like a holy terror!'

'Then just enjoy the rest of the summer,' said Tommy. 'We've nearly a month left.'

'I have a suggestion,' said Annie. 'You know my da drives a Model T?'

'Yes,' said Peter, his interest aroused. 'What about it?'

'He offered to take us all for a jaunt some Sunday when he's not working. We could go for a picnic if you wanted. Up in the mountains or to the seaside.'

'Brilliant,' said Susie.

'Yeah, that would be great,' agreed Tommy.

Annie looked at Peter.

'A jaunt in a Model T? Count me in!'

Annie seemed pleased at the enthusiastic reaction to her suggestion. 'OK, I'll ask him to do it the first Sunday he's free.'

'That's a deal then,' said Peter. He had never met Annie's father and he was eager to see what he was like. And he loved the idea of a chauffeur-driven trip to wherever the gang chose!

'Deal,' said Susie.

'Deal,' echoed Tommy.

Annie smiled and nodded. 'Deal.'

'Right,' said Peter, 'this calls for more lemonade.' Then he rose, took up the tray and made for the kitchen, his worries forgotten for now.

★ ★ ★

'I'm not your maid!' said Annie.

Her brother Sean looked up, his face showing surprise at her challenge.

The family had had a fry-up for tea, and now that they were finished, Ma was over at the sink cleaning pans. Da had sat back in his chair and begun to read the newspaper, and Annie had been about to go and get her library book when Sean had said, 'clear the table, Annie, will you, I want to do my football coupons.'

He said it as though it was entirely reasonable for her to do his bidding, and as he looked at her now, his initial surprise gave way to irritation. 'It wouldn't kill you to move a few cups and saucers,' he said.

'I worked longer hours in the shop than you did in the foundry,' answered Annie.

'Maybe we should give you a medal,' said Sean sarcastically. 'What have you done now, six weeks work?'

'I'm actually there eight weeks.'

'Bully for you.'

'It shouldn't matter how long I'm there. We're both working. If you want to do your coupons, why can't you clear the table yourself?'

'Oh, for God's sake!' said Sean, crossly.

Ma turned round from the sink and looked at Annie in appeal. 'It's not worth fighting about, love.'

I hate when she does that, thought Annie. Mrs Reilly didn't like arguments and was the peacemaker in the family, but Annie felt that asking her to be the one to give in wasn't fair. If it wasn't worth fighting about, why couldn't she have asked *Sean* to do it? Annie hesitated, trying to decide what to do. She didn't want to argue with her mother. If she did, Ma would probably say that she would clear the table herself when she was finished at the sink, and then Annie would feel bad. But she didn't want Sean to get away with lording it over her either. Before she got a chance to respond, Da put down his newspaper.

'Annie's right, Sean,' he said. 'She's putting in long hours as well. If you want the table for your football coupons, get off your backside and clear it yourself!'

Annie could see that Sean was really annoyed, but he wouldn't disobey his father. Da didn't usually get involved in disputes like this, but when he *did* make a ruling his word was final. Sean breathed out loudly to show his irritation, but he began clearing the table. Ma diplomatically went back to the pans without another word, and Da immersed himself again behind his newspaper. Annie was tempted to put her tongue out at her brother, but she told herself that that would be childish, and besides, she had won this particular battle.

She was about to rise from the table, but her eye was caught by an item on the opened page of her father's newspaper. *Rebels raid Dundalk*, the headline said, and Annie quickly scanned the article. It appeared that a large force of rebels had recently occupied the County Louth town, before it was re-taken by the army. The moment that she read it, Annie thought of Peter. Dundalk was the town from which he had travelled by train on his way home from Carlingford. She was really glad that his holiday had ended before the rebels had raided the town. Who knows what foolhardy thing Peter might have done had he become caught up in that chaos? Sometimes she worried about him. He was firmly on the side of the rebels, and he was impulsive and daring by nature. Annie hoped that the combination wouldn't land him in trouble. Before she could think any further about it she heard the hall door slamming, then Eamon burst into the room, his face ashen.

'Have you heard?!' he cried.

Eamon hadn't been with them for tea because he was doing overtime, and Annie wondered what awful news he had heard in work.

'Heard what?' said Ma nervously.

'About Michael Collins?'

'What about Collins?' asked Sean, his annoyance of a moment before clearly forgotten.

'He's been shot!' said Eamon. 'He was ambushed in West Cork.'

Annie was shocked. Even though Michael Collins was the Commander-in-Chief of the new army – and therefore, in theory, an enemy to all rebels – he was still admired on all sides because of his leading role in the War of Independence. 'Is he … is he going to be OK?' she asked.

Eamon shook his head. 'No. He's dead. They've shot Michael Collins dead.'

'You're certain?' said Da, his voice unsteady. 'It's not … it's not a rumour?'

'I wish it was. But a doctor confirmed it – he was pronounced dead.'

'God almighty,' said Da. He lowered his head into his hands, then looked up and spoke softly. 'It's really going to be savage now.'

Annie thought the war was savage already. But something in her father's tone made her fearful for the future, and though she couldn't say why, she felt a shiver run up her spine.

CHAPTER FOURTEEN

━━ ━━ ━━ ━━ ━━

It was the biggest crowd that Peter had ever seen. It was as if every man, woman and child in Dublin had spilled out onto the city streets for the funeral of Michael Collins. Peter's father had spoken to a police officer who said the crowd was estimated at half a million people – a staggering figure, and twenty per cent of the population of the entire country.

The whole city seemed to be in mourning, and throngs of people dressed in black crowded the centre of town when Peter, his parents, and his brother and sister had arrived by tram and made their way to Sackville Street. Peter was a little surprised by his parents' decision to attend the funeral. There had been a huge outpouring of grief, however, that Collins should be dead at just thirty-one years of age, and for the three days that Collins's remains had lain in state in City Hall large numbers of Dubliners had filed past to pay their respects. Peter's parents had originally been against the War of Independence, in which Collins had played a leading role, and Peter thought it showed how much they had changed that they were now mourning the death of the gunman-turned-statesman.

He had never discussed this with his parents – he couldn't really – but he wondered if their changed stance was mostly about looking after their own interests. Now that the Free State was a reality, it suited people to support the new powers-that-be. It even explained why his parents allowed him to attend the Irish language club, as though by having their son fluent in the Irish language they were showing their patriotic allegiance to the new state.

Or was he being too hard on them? Maybe they were just genuinely saddened, as so many people seemed to be, at the loss of a leader who had paid the highest price for his cause. Peter himself felt a bit confused today. He had been delighted when Finbar had recently made contact again, and he had delivered several secret messages, conveying orders from Mr Mac to rebel sympathisers in various parts of the city. He had also offered to store more contraband in his hiding place in the Botanics if necessary, and Mr Mac had thanked him and said they would let him know. And yet, despite the pride he took in working with the rebels, he couldn't shake off a sense of sadness to think that his former hero was dead.

He watched the funeral cortege making its approach up Sackville Street. The broad thoroughfare was crowded with onlookers along its entire length, but Peter had managed to work his way a little ahead of his family and had a good view down the street. He could hear the mournful sound of the 'Dead March' being played by a brass band, then he saw the funeral carriage coming into view. Six perfectly groomed horses pulled a gun carriage on which Collins's coffin lay draped in the national flag, the tricolour.

The cortege moved solemnly forward and Peter saw that behind the gun carriage were marching lines of army officers, their boots gleaming and their uniforms resplendent. Further back in the procession was a series of cars, each one laden with countless wreaths of flowers, and further back again there were honour guards of policemen and rifle-bearing soldiers, all marching solemnly and stony-faced behind the horse-drawn carriage.

As the flag-draped coffin drew nearer, people around Peter began to react. Some had tears in their eyes, some blessed themselves, others simply lowered their heads respectfully. Peter hadn't thought out what his response should be. Collins had, after all, been the commander of the Free State army, and as such was the enemy. But somehow, he didn't feel like the enemy. And especially not today.

The carriage drew level, and Peter hesitated before blessing himself reverently. Then it hit him that Michael Collins, the youthful, dashing hero that he had once idolised, was really dead. His emotions took him by surprise, and despite everything, tears welled up in his eyes, then rolled slowly down his cheeks.

✱ ✱ ✱

Annie ran across the beach and plunged into the water with a shriek. It was a glorious day in early September – sunny, warm, and without a hint of a breeze – but still, the waters of the Irish Sea made her gasp. Peter and Tommy followed closely behind, quickly wading out to find their depth, then diving in. The last of the gang into the sea was Susie, who hesitated with the water at waist height.

Annie turned around and called to her. 'Come on, Susie!'

'I will, just give me a chance to get used to it!'

No sooner had she said this than Tommy and Peter turned in

unison and began to splash her.

'No!' cried Susie.

'Scaredycat!' said Tommy, splashing her even more.

'Careful, Susie, you'll get wet!' called Peter in mock warning as he splashed her vigorously.

'I hope you're both swept out on a current!' cried Susie, then she launched herself into the water with an even louder shriek than Annie's.

Annie smiled at the antics of her friends, then did a fast Australian crawl parallel to the shoreline before turning around and floating on her back.

They had gone to the seaside at the Hole in the Wall, a tucked-away beach that was about eight miles outside Dublin and whose sands bordered the sea opposite the scenic island of Ireland's Eye. Da had suggested it as a location for their day out in the Model T, and as soon as they arrived, everyone had agreed that it was a good choice, and Da had retired to a sand dune to read his Sunday paper.

The trip itself had been difficult to organise, and several weeks had passed before they could find a Sunday that suited everyone. Today, however, had worked out well, what with the glorious sunshine and clear blue skies, and the fact that everyone had needed their spirits lifted after the recent funeral of Michael Collins. They would all be back in school next week, so she had been looking forward to today, knowing it would be the last gathering of summer.

It should have been a great day out, and in some ways it was, but Annie still felt a bit uncomfortable. While Susie had visited her house several times, today was the first time that Da had met Peter and Tommy. The boys had been courteous and friendly to her father, but to Annie's surprise, Da hadn't been his normal self. Instead of being relaxed, he had been over-polite and had tried too hard to impress her friends.

Annie loved him the way he was and found it embarrassing when he attempted to put on a front. While chatting to Peter and Tommy he had deliberately tried to use big words, but in a way that sounded unnatural, and Annie sensed that Peter had picked up on it. Peter was too well bred to show that he had noticed, but Annie couldn't help but wince all the same. She loved her father, and knew it wasn't Da's fault that he hadn't had the education she was getting, which made her ashamed of herself for feeling embarrassed.

Just then, she felt splashing as a swimmer approached, and she lifted her head to see who it was.

'God, how can the sea be freezing when the day's roasting?' exclaimed Susie as she drew near and treaded water.

It was the kind of remark that was typical of her friend, and Annie had to smile. She really should be more like Susie, and spend less time worrying about things. 'It's not that bad when you get used to it,' she answered.

'Yeah,' said Susie, 'it goes from freezing to just being cold! But listen, I've a great idea.'

'What?'

'I have to get my own back on the boys for splashing me. Why don't we swim in and hide their towels?'

Annie hesitated a moment, then she remembered her resolve to be more like her carefree friend and she nodded. 'Good idea. Race you in!' she cried, then she launched into the crawl again and swam for the shore.

***

Peter lay stretched out on the grass on the summit of Howth Head, savouring the spectacular view across Dublin Bay. They had spent most of the afternoon at the beach in the Hole in the Wall, then Annie's father had driven them to the top of Howth Head to have their picnic. Peter had enjoyed sitting in the front seat of the Model T with Mr Reilly, the warm summer breeze blowing in through the car's open windows as they drove through the fishing village of Howth, and up to the grassy slopes of the summit area, the highest point on the peninsula.

It had been a perfect summer's day, and now the sun was low in the sky, bathing the nearby hills and the waters of the bay in soft golden light. The distant mountains were silhouetted against a sky that was a beautiful hazy purple, a colour so striking that it reminded Peter of the lighting effects he had seen onstage when his family had gone to pantomimes in the Gaiety Theatre.

Mr Reilly sat by the car smoking his pipe, and Peter half listened as Annie, Susie and Tommy packed away the picnic things and chatted about popular songs.

' "Don't Dilly-Dally on the Way" is a brilliant song,' said Tommy.

'Isn't it?' said Annie. 'And I really love "I'm Forever Blowing Bubbles".'

'Yeah, but it's kind of stupid,' said Tommy. 'Like, why would anyone want to be always blowing bubbles?'

'It's just a song, Tommy,' said Susie. 'I mean, why would anyone want to dilly-dally for that matter?'

'There could be loads of reason why you'd want to dilly-dally,' said Tommy.

'Oh, for goodness sake!' exclaimed Susie. 'You'd argue—'

'With your toe-nails!' said Annie, finishing the sentence for her.

'Well, he would!' said Susie, joining in the laughter.

Annie looked really happy when she laughed, but Peter suspected that her life was much harder than his own. Meeting her father had been something of an eye-opener. Peter had really liked Mr Reilly, who had been friendly and eager to make the day's outing special, but it had made Peter realise that Annie's family were what his mother would call 'working class'. He guessed that Annie must have studied really hard to get the scholarship for Eccles Street, and he knew that all summer she had put in long hours at the fishmongers to raise cash for her family. It seemed unfair to Peter that dull, lazy children from rich families could just waltz into private schools, while someone bright like Annie had to overcome all sorts of problems. Before he could give it any more thought, however, Tommy called him.

'Take it easy there, Peter,' he said sarcastically, 'we'll carry the picnic stuff back to the car ourselves.'

Peter had been lost in his thoughts and he realised now that Mr Reilly was beating out the ashes from his pipe and that the others were rising to return to the Model T.

'A bit of work will do you good,' Peter retorted lightly, then he got up and took one final look across the bay. The light was even more magical now, and he could see Bray Head, the Sugar-loaf Mountain and the Wicklow Hills, their outlines softened by the purple evening light. Gazing down the cliffs he could see the Bailey Lighthouse on a dramatic outcrop of rock, looking like a sentinel guarding the entrance to the waters of the bay. Several small yachts, with white sails, were making for harbour. All in all, the scene was like a picture postcard or a beautiful landscape painting.

Peter had never before seen Dublin Bay looking so peaceful. But the coming weeks and months were *not* going to be peaceful, and so he stared at the scene now, wanting to store the image in his memory. Then he started after his friends, sorry to have to leave this perfect day behind, and to return once more to real life in the city.

CHAPTER FIFTEEN

___ ___ ___ ___

'Half way through, thank God!' whispered Susie to Annie, as the school bell rang to indicate lunch break.

It was the first day of term in Eccles Street and they were sharing a desk in a bright, airy classroom. How different it was from her old school, St Mary's, where the floors were covered in worn linoleum and the desk tops bore the carved initials of generations of pupils from the surrounding streets. Apart from the fact that her surroundings now were much nicer, Annie also found that secondary school was very different to primary school, with interesting new subjects like Latin and Science that she had never done in St Mary's. They had already had one Latin class this morning, and although Susie had bemoaned learning a language that nobody spoke anymore, Annie had enjoyed the class and liked the logical way that Latin worked.

It was good being a student here, she thought. In St Mary's it had been accepted that most pupils would leave school once they reached the age of thirteen or fourteen, and few people had much ambition beyond that. Here, though, there was an attitude that learning was important in its own right, and Annie was determined to grasp every opportunity the new school provided.

However, it was obvious, even on the first day, that cliques were developing. Several slightly snooty-looking girls who had attended primary school here were already forming a mini-unit in the class. Susie said not to worry about that, and insisted that she and Annie would make lots of other friends and that everything would be fine.

Annie hoped that Susie was right, but she was still aware that the other students were fee-paying, while she was here on a scholarship. She remembered Sister Josephine referring to her as the 'scholarship girl' during the open day. She had been nervous meeting their Year Head again this morning, and had hoped that the nun wouldn't draw attention to the scholarship and make her feel like the odd girl out.

Sister Josephine had greeted her pleasantly, though Annie had felt a bit on edge when the nun said she remembered her from their last meeting. To her relief, Sister Josephine had made no reference to the scholarship, and had simply welcomed her once more to Eccles Street. Annie had told herself not to get obsessed about fitting in, and to just try and relax, like Susie did.

They were about to leave the classroom for the lunchtime break, when Sister Immaculata swept into the room and clapped her hands for attention.

'One moment, girls, before you have lunch,' said the older nun, and all of the pupils stopped what they were doing. Sister Immaculata looked around the room, waiting until she had complete silence. 'All of you will be starting sports tomorrow afternoon,' she said. 'Now, some of you will already be familiar with our facility in Shandon Park, but for those who weren't in our junior school, let me tell you something important.'

Annie listened attentively. Susie had already played quite a bit of tennis and hockey, but Annie had experienced no organised sports in St Mary's, where there had been just chasing and skipping in the school yard.

'Once every week you will make your way to Phibsboro, for camogie in Shandon Park,' said Sister Immaculata.

This sounded good to Annie. Camogie was the girls' version of hurling, almost like hockey, only more full-blooded. Annie had sometimes played it on the road with her friends, but she looked forward to playing it properly now on a real pitch at Shandon Park.

Sister Immaculata looked from girl to girl as though challenging anyone not to give her their full attention, then she continued. 'When you travel each week to Phibsboro, you will do three things. One, you will travel in good time so as not to be late; two, you will have your full kit with you, properly cleaned since the last match. And three – can anyone tell me what the third requirement is?'

'That we won't arrive drunk!' whispered Susie.

Annie wanted to smile, but even though Sister Immaculata wasn't looking their way, she forced herself not to.

'That we behave like ladies, Sister,' said one of the snooty-faced girls.

'Quite so, Ethel,' replied Sister Immaculata, nodding approvingly to the girl before turning back to the rest of the class. 'When you travel on the public roads, be it to Shandon Park or to any other sporting fixture, you represent this school. You don't shout, you don't scream, you don't engage in horseplay with your sporting equipment. You comport yourselves like young ladies. Understood?'

'Yes, Sister,' answered the girls in chorus.

'Good. In the event that any girl fails to do so, it will be severely dealt with. Is that also understood?'

'Yes, Sister.'

'Very good. Thank you for your attention. You may now break for lunch.' The nun turned and quickly exited the room.

Susie breathed out exaggeratedly. 'Whew, bit of a dragon, isn't she?'

'Pretty scary all right,' answered Annie.

'Do you know the answer to that?'

'No, what?'

'Imagine her in her pyjamas,' said Susie.

'What?'

'That's what my dad always says,' she answered with a grin. 'If someone is all cross and important-looking, you imagine them in their pyjamas, and then they don't seem half as frightening!'

Annie laughed.

'Well it's true, isn't it?!'

'I think even in her pyjamas she'd be scary!' answered Annie, but she had to admit that the image Susie had conjured up of the vice-principal in her pyjamas did diminish the nun's forbidding aura.

'Come on, let's have lunch,' said Susie.

'Right,' said Annie and they started for the door. 'I'm really looking forward to the camogie, are you?'

'Yeah,' said Susie, then she lowered her voice and indicated the girl who had answered the vice-principal's question. 'And when we get your woman Ethel and her stuck-up friends on the pitch, we'll hack the legs off them!'

Annie laughed again, then she headed off to have lunch with

Susie, pleased with her first morning in the new school, and looking forward to being a pupil here.

★ ★ ★

Peter felt excited. It was always a thrill to be on a mission, and tonight he was cycling along a fog-covered country road en route to meet Ned Morgan, the owner of Willow Cottage. He imagined that this was what it must have been like serving in the flying columns that used to strike suddenly against the Black and Tans, then disappear into the countryside during the guerrilla warfare of the War of Independence. Guerrilla warfare was going to be the way of the future, now that the main cities had all been re-taken by the army. Peter believed, however, that the rebels could make the country ungovernable. Then they could force the government to re-negotiate the treaty with Britain, and so still acquire a full republic.

This morning he had received a request from Mr Mac to move another consignment of contraband from the cottage to the hiding place in the Botanical Gardens. It was fairly urgent, the schoolteacher had said – breaking his normal rule by calling Peter aside in Belvedere – as the government forces were frequently raiding the homes and farms of suspected rebel sympathisers. Peter had promised to do it tonight, and the timing had been good, with his mother caught up in her Friday bridge night, and his father in Cork at a dental conference. His older sister and brother usually went into town on Friday nights and so Peter had been able to slip out unnoticed.

He cycled along Ballyboggan Road now, the front light on his bicycle barely illuminating the foggy route ahead. When he had left Glasnevin, the fog had been lighter, but here in the country-side it had grown thicker, and he had to cycle more slowly.

He rounded a bend, and being familiar with the route, he realised that he wasn't too far from Cardiffs Bridge. He contin-ued on through the fog and saw faintly visible lights at the next bend on the road. He heard the soft rumble of engines turning over, then the sound ceased as first one engine, then another was turned off. Peter braked at once, immediately on the alert. Lorries travelling at this hour of the evening might very well be taking part in a raid.

Peter dismounted, then proceeded quietly on foot, anxious to see what was going on. He felt his pulse beginning to race and the thought occurred to him that if the lorries really were part of a raid, it was highly likely that Willow Cottage was the target. The smart course of action would be to slip away now to avoid a trap. But if the lorries really were full of soldiers about to launch a raid, did he not have a duty to try and warn his comrades?

He stood there a moment, uncertain what to do, then made up his mind. He would find out if the lorries were military vehicles before deciding anything. He switched off his lights and walked gingerly ahead, wheeling the bicycle. He was glad now of the ever- thickening fog and the lack of other traffic on the road at this hour of the evening.

Drawing nearer, he felt his heart sink. Both vehicles were army trucks. He could faintly make out the outline of a man standing at the cab of the nearest vehicle, then he heard his voice.

'It's not marked on the map,' said the soldier, 'but there's sup-posed to be a turn before the bridge.'

That settled it, thought Peter; the army was preparing to raid the cottage. He stepped back into the fog for fear that the soldier might look up from the map and see him. He knew he had had a near miss and that he should get out of here fast. If he fled now, though, the soldiers would catch Ned red-handed with whatever weapons he had ready for Peter to take away.

Could he get to the cottage first and warn him? He definitely couldn't risk trying to cycle past the army lorries. But supposing he ran unseen across the fields? It might be possible to get there ahead of the troops. It was a big risk and there was no telling what would happen if it back-fired and he was captured. Or worse, he could be shot during the raid – things like that happened all the time. The thought of being shot really frightened him, but he hated the idea of slinking off home and leaving Ned to be captured. He weighed up his choices, then acted impulsively.

Moving quickly but quietly, he wheeled the bicycle back to a gate he had passed. On the other side of the gate were fields that led down to the river, and without hesitating any further, he hoisted the bicycle up in the air and lowered it down on the other side of the gate. He swiftly climbed over the gate and slipped off the bicycle's front lamp. Then he hid the bike where he could retrieve it later, resting it out of sight behind the hedgerow. The fog was even thicker towards the river Tolka, but Peter knew these fields well from his many picnics here. Using the bicycle lamp to pick out a route, he made his way down the sloping field towards the river as quickly as he could.

He took care not to shine the light in the direction of the road, and he prayed that the fog would prevent him from being spotted by the soldiers. Despite the cold night air, he was sweating, and the hair on the back of his neck stood on end when he thought of what it would be like to get a bullet in the back.

No shots were fired, however, and to his relief he reached a track that ran alongside the river. Picking up his pace, he ran through the swirling fog. Even with the poor visibility he knew exactly where he was now, and before reaching Cardiffs Bridge he cut left across a pasture, quickly scaled a gate and dropped down onto the road.

He ran up the lane leading to Willow Cottage, hit the latch on the front door and burst into the living room.

'God almighty!' cried Ned, as he spun round from where he was sitting at the table.

The older man had been drinking tea from an enamel mug and some of the tea had splashed onto his shirt with the shock of Peter's sudden arrival. There wasn't time for apologies or explanations however, and Peter spoke rapidly.

'You're going to be raided!'

'How do you know—?'

'The army are just up the road!' cried Peter, cutting him short.

Just then the sound of revving engines could be heard.

'That's them!' said Peter. 'Have you got the stuff for me?!'

'Yes,' said Ned, overcoming his initial shock and rising swiftly from the table. He went to a wicker basket full of sods of turf. He reached under the top sods and pulled out a package sealed with sacking and thrust it into Peter's hands.

Peter could hear the sound of the trucks changing gear and he knew they were coming down the nearby hill, but he forced himself not to panic.

'Have you anything else they shouldn't find?' he asked.

'No, that's it. You run out the back, through the barn, I'll brazen it out here.'

'Right.'

'Good luck, son! Run like the wind!'

Ned opened the back door of the kitchen, and Peter ran down a passageway, through another door and into the barn. He heard the sound of the trucks pulling into the lane, then skidding to a halt at the front of the cottage. There were shouts and whistles being blown, but he concentrated on finding the rear door of the barn, using the beam from his bicycle lamp. He heard the door of the cottage being kicked open just as he stepped out the back of the barn into the fog-enshrouded night. He was now on the side of the barn furthest from the cottage's front entrance, but he was still only a short distance away from the shouting soldiers.

His heart pounded so heavily that his chest felt like it was going to burst, but he resisted the temptation to flee. Ned had said to run like the wind, but that wasn't possible in the fog. And running through the farmyard might well alert the soldiers, some of whom he heard fanning out around the cottage. Instead, he switched off the lamp and slowly stepped backwards into the shelter of an apple orchard. He eased back as deeply as he could into the apple trees, being careful not to snap any fallen branches. Suddenly, two soldiers burst out of the rear door of the barn, one of them carrying a lantern. Peter could make out their shape in the thick fog, but he hoped that by standing immobile in the dark and the fog he would not be seen.

He heard angry voices from the cottage, then Ned cried out, presumably having been struck a blow. Peter hoped they wouldn't mistreat him any further, then his thoughts were turned to self

138

preservation. The soldier carrying the lantern was moving up the yard, drawing closer to Peter's hiding place. Peter's every instinct was to draw away, but he knew that any movement would be a mistake. Instead he held his breath, hoping the soldier wouldn't spot him in the heavy, swirling mist.

The solder stopped. 'Here, Paddy,' he said. 'Guess what I've found.'

Peter felt his mouth go dry. *Was the man playing cat and mouse with him?*

'What is it?' said the other soldier.

'Something that means we haven't wasted our time.'

'I can't see anything,' said the second soldier.

'I can, though.'

Peter felt his knees trembling and he pressed them together.

'What is it?' repeated the second soldier.

'Something you find in orchards. Apples!'

Peter watched in disbelief as the lantern-holder plucked an apple off one of the trees and threw it to his friend. 'Here,' he cried laughingly, 'spoils of war!' Then he plucked another apple for himself before both men turned away and headed back into the barn.

Peter felt a wave of relief and he breathed out deeply but silently. *Time to get out of here,* he thought. He didn't like leaving Ned with the enemy soldiers, but the older man had said there was nothing else illegal in the house, so he should be all right.

The soldiers would probably turn the cottage upside down searching for contraband, which meant they would be there for a quite a while. All he had to do now was retreat deeper into the fog and make his way through the fields parallel to the road. Once he was well away from the cottage he would regain the road and run back to where he had hidden his bicycle. All going well, he would be back in Glasnevin before the soldiers had to admit that there was nothing to be found. He breathed out deeply again, his relief giving way to exhilaration, then he grasped the precious parcel for which he had come and disappeared deeper into the trees.

CHAPTER SIXTEEN

■ ■ ■ ■

Annie was fascinated to see her friends' parents in party mood. Peter's family held a musical evening several times each year, to which friends, neighbours and relatives were invited, and this was Annie's first time to attend. She loved the festive atmosphere tonight in Botanic Lodge, the Scanlon's large rambling home. It seemed wonderfully warm and welcoming, through a magical combination of candlelight, roaring log fires, and large quantities of delicious food and drink. The entertainment had been lively too, and Annie had been surprised to discover that Mrs Scanlon was the kind of pianist who could move easily from playing Chopin to accompanying singers who did light-hearted Percy French songs, like 'Phil the Fluter's Ball'.

Annie had always found Mrs Scanlon to be pleasant without actually being warm, but tonight she saw a more relaxed version of her friend's mother. Susie and Tommy's father, Mr O'Neill, was performing now, and this too was revealing. Annie had often encountered him around his vet's surgery while visiting Susie, and he had always been friendly, but tonight he was showing a more dramatic side to his nature. He was singing the ballad 'Love Thee Dearest, Love Thee', and was performing full-bloodedly, his hand clutched dramatically to his heart as he sang to Susie's smiling mother in a strong tenor voice. Annie thought to herself that she now knew where Susie got her outgoing manner.

Annie had put on her best outfit for tonight and had worn new silk ribbons in her hair. She was glad that she had, because all of the other children present – most of them cousins of Peter's – were beautifully dressed. None of them had been stand-offish though, and Annie had mixed easily with them, and had even got a loud cheer from all of the children when she had sung her party piece, 'Are you right there, Michael?'

She rose now to go to the bathroom, slipping quietly out into the hall without distracting Mr O'Neill, who was working up to a crescendo. Her friends were enjoying the company of Peter's cousins, and it struck Annie that her absence wouldn't be noticed for a while. She was tempted by the idea of exploring Peter's home, having only ever been in the sitting room and the kitchen on her previous visits. The house was really grand compared to her own, and was full of interesting corners. But even though she was curious and could have done a little discreet snooping now without being detected, she told herself that she was a guest and that this would be bad manners.

Instead she crossed the hallway and entered the downstairs toilet. It was surprisingly spacious and Annie was impressed by the sweet-smelling bowl of potpourri on the window ledge and the tall pink wax candles that augmented the soft gas lighting.

After using the toilet, she washed her hands with a lavender scented soap and then dried them in a soft, fluffy towel. *This is the way to live!* she thought.

While washing her hands she had heard a telephone ringing, and when she stepped back into the hallway, she was surprised to see Peter standing at its far end with his back to her. He had the telephone cradled to his ear and was speaking in a serious, urgent voice that Annie could just make out over the background noise of the party.

'I suppose I could get it now if you really need it,' he said.

Annie's instincts told her that something important was happening, and she stood stock still, wanting to hear more.

'OK, if it's urgent I will,' said Peter in answer to whatever the caller had requested. 'All right, but don't come down on a motorbike. I'll meet you at the corner in a few minutes.'

Annie was intrigued, but worried too. Peter's allegiances were with the rebels. *Was he getting involved in something illegal?* It sounded like it, and when he hung up and made for the kitchen without a backward glance, she found herself following him. Annie didn't know what exactly was going on, but she sensed that her friend was doing something risky, and without thinking it through, she decided to find out.

Peter opened the French windows and stepped out into the garden. Annie waited a moment, then followed suit. She had no idea where she was going or what she would say if he turned around and caught her. He seemed to be completely intent on what he was about, however, and in the hazy moonlight Annie saw him striding towards the far end of the garden.

She followed at a distance, confident that she wouldn't be seen from the house, where the curtains were drawn on all the windows. She saw Peter reaching the boundary wall of the garden. The Scanlons' house backed onto the Botanical Gardens, and Annie was intrigued when she saw Peter bending down low, lifting away a sheet of wood, then squeezing though a hidden gap in the bars of the boundary wall. So he had a hidden entrance into the Bots! But what on earth was he up to?

She waited a moment to let him get clear, then quickly crossed to the garden boundary herself. She hitched up her dress, not wanting to soil her best outfit, then she crouched down and silently moved the sheet of wood that Peter had replaced. She squeezed through the bars as quickly as she could, not wanting to lose sight of Peter in the darkened grounds.

She heard movement up ahead, then caught a glimpse of him in the moonlight as he followed a faintly visible path. Annie looked across the gloomy expanse of the Botanical Gardens and hesitated. On the other side of the gardens was Glasnevin Cemetery, where Michael Collins had been buried just a few weeks ago. It was a really spooky place that still featured watch towers that had been built to discourage grave-robbers. This really wasn't somewhere she wanted to go. But she was very worried about Peter, and so she forced herself to master her fears and set off along the path after him. She moved as quickly as she could in the moonlight, her night vision improving now that she was away from the lights of the house. Suddenly she stepped on a twig. It snapped with a crack.

Annie stopped dead and flattened herself against a large tree. Peter must have heard the noise because the faint sound of his footsteps had halted. Annie stood stock still, praying that he would assume the noise had been made by an animal. Would a fox or a badger be heavy enough to snap a twig? She had no idea. Or would he sense the presence of another person, would the hairs rise on his neck the way they sometimes did when you felt you were being observed by someone unseen? Her mind racing, she stood there, holding her breath and dreading the thought of Peter silently backtracking and catching her.

After a moment, though, she heard him moving off again and she breathed out quietly, then set off after him. As it happened, she didn't have much further to go, and up ahead she saw Peter going around the back of what looked like a storage shed. Annie suspected that she must be in some sort of maintenance area, then before she could give it further thought, Peter emerged from behind the shed, carrying something in his hands.

To Annie's surprise, he didn't retrace his steps towards the house but made his way further along the path. Keeping as far behind him as possible without losing him from sight, Annie followed. He continued along the path that now veered right, which Annie realised was bringing them back in the general direction of Peter's house, but towards what must be one of the side entrances to the Botanical Gardens.

Keeping to the shadows, Annie trailed him, then saw that he was opening a latch on a pedestrian door built into the gate. He swung the door open and Annie saw a dim street light on the far side of the gate. Peter stepped out and closed the wicket gate after him.

Now alone in the dark, Annie didn't want to linger, and she quickly made for the wicket gate, waited a moment to allow Peter to have walked on, then opened the gate and stepped out on the street. She gently closed the gate after her and looked ahead, suddenly getting her bearings. They were at the far end of the laneway on which Peter's house was located, and Peter was striding towards the corner of the much more brightly lit main thoroughfare at Botanic Road.

Annie could hear a motorcycle engine gently turning over, and she remembered Peter's telephone conversation. Clearly he was about to deliver the hidden parcel to the motorcyclist, and Annie guessed that the parcel's contents had to be illegal.

Peter was about halfway up the laneway when there was a commotion at the corner of the main road. Annie saw several men approaching the motorcyclist, whose engine immediately roared to life. She watched the motorcyclist careening across the head of the laneway and handing off one of the men who had tried to grab him. The motorcyclist mounted the footpath, and Annie caught a glimpse of its helmet-clad rider pushing the other man to the ground, then the engine roared again and the bike sped away.

Peter froze for a moment, then Annie saw him swiftly moving to the boundary wall of his garden and tossing the parcel over the wall. He turned on his heel, then stopped in amazement on seeing Annie.

'Annie?! What … what are you doing here?'

'I could ask the same,' she said.

Peter looked completely taken aback. 'Let's … let's get out of here first,' he said.

He indicated the way back to the wicket gate, but before they could walk away, two of the men who had tried to apprehend the motorcyclist started up the laneway.

'You there. Not so fast!'

Annie's pulse had been racing, but her heart began thumping even faster when the men drew near and identified themselves as detectives. Both were tall and heavily built, and the older of the two, a stern-faced man with a grey moustache, seemed to be in charge.

'What are you doing here?' he asked Peter, his tone aggressive.

'I live here,' said Peter.

'Really? Where exactly?'

'That house there, Botanic Lodge. We're having a party.'

'Except you're not at the party, you're out here. And so was someone else we'd like to talk to.'

'I don't know anything about that,' said Peter.

Annie was impressed by Peter's coolness, but she knew he would be in huge trouble if he couldn't convince the policemen, and if they searched the house and gardens.

'What's your name?' said the man.

'Peter Scanlon.'

'And you?'

'Annie Reilly,' she answered, trying to keep her voice from sounding shaky.

The second policeman looked at Peter. 'Good party, is it?' he queried.

'Yes, very good,' replied Peter.

'Then why weren't you in at it?'

Peter hesitated, and the older man looked at him piercingly.

'What were you doing out here?' he insisted.

'I was…'

'What?'

'We were dared,' answered Peter, pointing at Annie.

'Dared?'

'To play sweethearts.'

'What's that?'

'It's … it's a game where you're dared to go down the lane here and … and kiss a girl in the dark,' said Peter with embarrassment.

'Bit young for that, aren't you?' asked the second man.

'It's ... it's just a game.'

The older man looked at Annie.

'Is this true?'

Annie had expected Peter to lie, but this explanation had taken her completely by surprise. If the police found the package and she was discovered to be lying she would be arrested. And if that happened she could lose her scholarship. All of Ma and Da's hard work and sacrificing, all of her own efforts would have been wasted. Peter shouldn't have put her on the spot, she thought angrily. He was asking her to take a huge risk. And it was all right for the Scanlons, they had money, so no matter what happened, Peter could always go to college. For her, though, there was only one opportunity, and to lose it would be a disaster.

'Well?' prompted the policeman.

Peter was trying to keep a brave face, but Annie could see that he was frightened. He was her friend and she didn't want to see him arrested, but could she risk everything?

The policeman was looking at her impatiently, and Annie knew she had to answer. 'Yes,' she said suddenly, 'it's true. We just came out for a minute and then ... then we got a fright when we heard the motorbike screaming off. That's all that happened. Can we go back in now, please?'

Annie held her breath. The priests who had visited her school had taught that a lie was always sinful, but nevertheless she prayed now that her lie would be believed.

The policeman looked at her appraisingly, then he nodded wearily. 'Go on then.'

'Thank you,' said Annie.

'And go easy with the kissing,' said the other man with a smirk. 'You're not much more than chisellers!'

The two men turned away and strode briskly back up the laneway as Annie and Peter made their way to the entrance to the house. They turned into the driveway, and once out of sight, Annie turned furiously on Peter.

'Peter Scanlon! What do you think you're doing?'

'I'm sorry, Annie. I didn't mean to drag you into it.'

'I'll lose everything if I'm arrested. My scholarship, Eccles Street, everything!'

'I'm sorry, I ... I was desperate, I just–'

'Just nothing! You could be in big trouble too. You're hiding stuff for the rebels, aren't you?'

Peter didn't answer at once.

'I know you are. I followed you into the Bots. I saw you throwing the stuff over the wall!'

'When did you become a spy?'

'When did you become a fanatic?'

'I'm not a fanatic.'

'You're risking lives in a war you can't win!'

'We have to fight on.'

'No! You don't.' Annie paused, calming down a little. She looked questioningly at Peter. 'Have you ever not got what you wanted?'

'Sorry?'

'You're so used to getting what you want, Peter. You've never had to settle for an old overcoat, or cheap shoes or a second hand bicycle, have you? And now your die-hard friends didn't get exactly what they wanted in the Treaty. So they're annoyed. Except they're not just annoyed, they're *killing people* because they're annoyed!'

Peter looked a bit taken aback, then he spoke softly. 'They're risking their own lives, Annie.'

'They're risking *everyone's* lives. That's what people like you do!'

'People like me?'

'People who don't have to worry. If you'd been caught, you'd be in trouble. If *I'm* caught, it's over, I lose everything. If the police find out what I did tonight, Peter, I'm finished.'

'They won't find out.'

'Supposing you're arrested over something else?'

'I'd never give your name. Never.'

'They could still link us. I couldn't bear to lose my scholarship now, Peter. Not after just four weeks in Eccles Street!'

Peter looked down and breathed out.

'I'm really sorry,' he said. 'I ... I didn't think about affecting you. I'm really sorry, Annie, for doing that to you.'

Annie looked at his downcast face and saw that he genuinely meant it. 'I couldn't inform on a friend,' she said. 'So I'll just pray we get away with this – and that you see sense. I'm going home now.'

Peter was about to respond, but Annie raised her hand and stopped him.

'Goodnight, Peter,' she said, then she turned and walked quickly away.

CHAPTER SEVENTEEN

━━ ━━ ━━ ━━ ━━

Peter was on his knees, his hands joined in prayer, as the priest made his way to the pulpit to deliver the sermon. Every Sunday morning Peter and his parents attended eleven o'clock Mass together, and for the couple of weeks since the incident with the police Peter had prayed hard that there wouldn't be any problems for Annie and her scholarship. So far, nothing more had come of it, however, and Peter gave thanks that his prayers seemed to have been answered.

After the incident, Mr Mac had sincerely apologised. The schoolteacher had explained that Finbar must have been under secret surveillance on the night in question, but that he had made good his getaway on the motorbike. Finbar had since gone into hiding, so the authorities wouldn't know what he had been doing at Botanic Road or whom he had planned to meet. Peter had been relieved to hear all of this, although it had still taken a couple of weeks before he felt confident that Annie was in the clear.

He had been afraid that the incident might affect their friendship, and there *had* been a slight tension between them when they met again, travelling to school with Susie and Tommy. It hadn't lasted too long, though, and as time had passed with no problems from the police, things between them had returned to normal.

There was still the matter of their different views on the civil war, of course. Annie's arguments had been passionately made, and he could see her point, but he still felt that on balance the rebels were in the right. They hadn't discussed it any further – sometimes it was best to agree to disagree – and he was happy just to be friends again.

Peter rose from his knees and sat back in the pew as Canon Dudley, their parish priest, mounted the pulpit to give his sermon. This was the part of the Mass that Peter liked least, but today the canon held an envelope in his hand, and Peter was curious as to what it might contain.

The priest stood facing his congregation, then spoke solemnly. 'My dear brethren, I have here a most important document that I wish to read to you.'

Peter listened more carefully than usual, sensing that something was afoot. The canon put on his reading glasses and removed the letter from the envelope. 'This is a statement from their lordships, the Bishops of Ireland,' he said, 'on the vexed question of the civil war.'

If Peter had been curious before, he was totally attentive now.

The older man held up the letter and began to read. There wasn't a sound to be heard in the church as Canon Dudley read out a condemnation of the anti-Treaty campaign.

'This campaign is a system of murder and assassination of the National forces and is without any legitimate authority,' said the canon. 'The guerrilla warfare now being carried out by the irregulars is without moral sanction, and the killing of National soldiers is murder before God, the seizing of public and private property is robbery, the breaking of roads, bridges and railways is criminal. All who are in contravention of this teaching and who participate in such crimes are guilty of grievous sins, and may not be absolved in confession nor admitted to the Holy Communion if they persist in such evil courses.'

Peter listened, horrified. How could the bishops be so biased? And how could they refuse confession and Holy Communion to people because of their political beliefs? All through the rest of Mass he struggled with his anger, then finally the service was over and he exited the church with his parents. There was an animated hubbub of conversation as the congregation emerged from the church, and Peter suspected that he wasn't the only one who was furious.

'That was a rather strong response from the bishops,' said his father.

'About time, too,' his mother said firmly.

Peter knew that he should say nothing, but he couldn't stay quiet. 'How does that make sense, Mum?' he said.

His mother looked at him in surprise. 'I beg your pardon?'

'At Michael Collins's funeral there were loads of priests walking behind the coffin. So how is it OK when Michael Collins fights for Ireland, but it's a sin when other people do?'

'Michael Collins was a member of the government, Peter.'

'Not when he was fighting the British, Mum. Then he was a guerrilla fighter. Like the men Canon Dudley says are committing a sin.'

Peter could see that his mother was irritated, but she kept her impatience in check.

'It's hardly your place to question the bishops, Peter. But since you *do*, Mr Collins's government was elected. That's the difference – the chasm – between the government forces and the irregulars.

Now, I don't want to hear any further questioning from you of Church teaching. Is that clear?'

'Yes, Mum,' said Peter, as they made their way towards the chapel gate. But it wasn't clear to him at all. This would be the wrong time to make a stand with his parents. But the fight would go on, and he wasn't giving in, bishops or no bishops.

★ ★ ★

Annie loved the sound of the rain lashing against the window panes. It was warm and cosy in the classroom, and she liked the sense of cheating the elements as she listened to the rain pelting down outside. In fact, she liked almost everything about the convent. She had even come to enjoy the elocution classes, about which she had been a bit wary at first. They were conducted by the Burke sisters, two specially hired lay teachers who came into the school and coached the girls on correct English pronunciation. Annie's accent was a little stronger than some of the other girls in the class, but she had been determined not to adopt a posh accent just because she had changed schools.

In time, though, she had actually come to look forward to the elocution classes, which most of the girls looked on as a break from normal school work. And she had decided that there was nothing wrong with working on correct pronunciation, as long as you didn't adopt a phoney accent – which she definitely wasn't going to do. After all, many of the nuns had country accents, including Sister Josephine and the daunting Sister Immaculata, and nobody seemed to think there was any problem with that.

Annie was wondering how people got accents in the first place when her reverie was broken as Sister Josephine turned from the blackboard and addressed the class.

'Can any girl tell me what the Latin word *flumen* means?'

Susie turned in the desk that she shared with Annie and raised an eyebrow, as if to say *you must be joking*. Annie gave a tiny smile in response, being careful not to let the nun see her.

Annie knew that *flumen* was the Latin word for a river, but she didn't raise her hand or give any indication that she had the answer. She was almost six weeks in Eccles Street now, and during that time she had gotten on good terms with most of her class-mates. There was a small minority of girls who were snooty and who looked down on Annie – and indeed on many of their other fellow pupils. Susie's joke was that they regarded themselves as the cream of the crop – and that, like cream, they were rich and thick.

Annie had come to realise that she would never win their approval and now she didn't bother trying. The rest of the girls were a different matter, though, and she was wary of appearing too clever at their expense. She fully intended excelling in her writ-ten exams, but no-one liked a pupil who showed off too much in the classroom, and so she resisted the temptation to raise her hand now.

Lilly Norton put up her hand eagerly. 'Is *flumen* the Latin word for the flu, Sister?' she asked.

'No, Lilly, it's not,' answered Sister Josephine patiently.

The nun looked around the class, briefly catching Annie's eye, but Annie looked away. She suspected that Sister Josephine knew that she sometimes chose not to show off her knowledge. But unlike Beanpole, her old teacher in St Mary's, who had never realised that holding a pupil up as a shining example could make her unpopular, Sister Josephine was sensitive, and if she knew that Annie sometimes held back, she didn't press the matter.

'Is it a river, Sister?' said Una Gannon.

'Well done, Una, it is, indeed, a river,' said the nun.

Susie turned to Annie and made a face. Everyone in the class knew that Una's father taught Latin and English for the Christian Brothers in O'Connell's School, and that he gave Una frequent grinds in Latin. Just then, the bell rang to indicate the end of class.

'Very well, girls,' said Sister Josephine. 'For the next day I want you all to conjugate the list of verbs I've given you.'

'Yes, Sister,' answered the class.

There was a general buzz of conversation, and Susie turned happily to Annie. 'Lunchtime in Ecland,' she said. 'Let's conjugate a few jam sandwiches!'

Annie and Susie rose from their desks. Suddenly, there was the sound of shots from the road outside, and many of the pupils rushed to the windows to see what was happening. Annie was just in time to see a rain-sodden man in civilian clothes running along the street below. He wore no hat, and his hair was plastered to his skull. He had a revolver in his hand, but despite the fact that he was armed and, presumably, dangerous, he had a pathetic, hunted look about him. He suddenly wheeled about and fired off another shot at the group of soldiers who were pursuing him, then he turned and sprinted down the road, zigzagging to avoid the return fire from the soldiers.

'Back from the windows, girls! Back immediately!' cried Sister Josephine.

Annie obeyed the nun. She heard three further shots, followed by silence, and wondered if the man had escaped or if the soldiers had shot him. Even though he was a rebel, and on the wrong side, in Annie's view, she couldn't help but feel sorry for him. He had looked so frantic as he was chased, and now perhaps he was dying on the cold wet pavement, and all because he had insisted on fighting on.

The image brought Peter to her mind, and she thought back to the night when he had almost been caught by the police. Fortunately for both of them, nothing further had come of it. But despite his apologies for involving her, she feared that her arguments hadn't swayed him. Neither of them had discussed it again, but she was almost sure that he would still be involved with the rebels – which meant that he could end up being hunted like the rain-soaked gunman. She thought of how much she liked Peter, and hoped against hope that she was wrong.

▬   ▬   ▬   ▬   ▬

CHAPTER EIGHTEEN

'This calls for a bit of brute force!' said Susie. 'Give us the hammer there, Tommy, will you?'

Tommy looked aghast at his twin sister. 'You don't hammer in a screw,' he said.

'You do when the screwdriver won't get it any further,' said Susie, then before he could protest, she took the hammer and delivered several firm blows to the wooden theatre flat on which she was working. 'Bingo!' said Susie, and Peter and Annie laughed at Tommy's look of disgust.

They were helping to make and decorate a set for a concert that the Irish club was planning, and while most of the other girls had concentrated on making costumes or painting the scenery, Susie had insisted that she wanted to help build the set.

Although, strictly speaking, all conversation at the club was supposed to be in Irish, the friends often slipped into English if Mr McMahon and the other adults running the club weren't there to overhear.

'You should stick to what you're able for,' said Tommy

'I'm well able for you anyway,' answered Susie.

'Why can't you be like other girls? Why do you always have to be different?'

'Why shouldn't she?' said Annie. 'Why shouldn't a girl help make the set?'

'Because it ends up with screws being hammered into wood!' said Tommy.

Annie thought that this was a weak argument. What was the point in the nuns in school encouraging them to be ambitious, if they were always going to be stopped from doing things?

'Times change, Tommy,' she said. 'A woman is after being made a senator in America.'

'So what?'

'So the whole world is changing, dummy!' said Susie.

'Says who?' persisted Tommy, though Annie suspected that the main reason he was taking this stance was so as not to be bested by his sister.

'It is, Tommy,' she said reasonably. 'They said a woman couldn't be elected to parliament, but Countess Markievicz proved them wrong. Didn't she, Peter?'

Peter hesitated, and Annie sensed that he didn't want to side with the girls against his friend. But picking Countess Markievicz had been a good choice. Despite being born an aristocrat, the countess had become a staunch republican who had fought in the war of independence, and who sided with rebels in the current civil war. It would be hard for someone like Peter to criticise her.

'Yeah, she did,' he admitted.

'And I bet there'll be women on this new radio station too,' said Susie.

Peter looked at her with interest. 'What radio station?'

'It's called the BBC,' said Susie. 'And even though it's in London, you'll be able to pick up the signal and hear it miles away.'

'Sister Claire told us all about it in science,' said Annie.

'Bully for her,' said Tommy. 'Anyway, Mr Mac is giving out lemonade in the kitchen,' he added, abruptly changing the subject and indicating the small kitchen at the far end of the meeting room.

'Do you want a glass?' he said to Peter.

'Yeah, thanks.'

'Here, I'll come with you, crosspatch,' said Susie. 'Do you want some lemonade, Annie?'

'Yes, please.'

The twins headed off, and Peter looked at Annie. 'She doesn't let him away with much, does she?' he said good-humouredly, then he picked up a screwdriver and returned to work on the set.

Annie watched him, wondering how to phrase what she wanted to say. She hadn't been alone with him since the incident the previous week when she had seen the gunman being hunted by the troops. It had played on her mind, and she looked at Peter now, then decided to take the plunge. 'Peter?'

'Yeah.'

'Are you still... ' she paused, trying to find the right words. 'I saw a man being shot at last week. The Army were chasing him, and he ... he might have been killed. I really hope you're not still ... doing things.'

'It's OK, Annie, I'm not going to be killed.'

'So you've stopped then?'

Peter didn't answer immediately, and Annie waited, wanting so much to hear him saying that he had stopped. Eventually he breathed out and looked her in the eye. 'You're a good friend, Annie, so I won't lie. And I won't involve you ever again, I promise you.'

Annie felt her heart sink. 'So you're still involved.'

'We're not going to agree on this. So the less said, the better. OK?'

Annie nodded reluctantly, and Peter nodded in return, then went back to work. But it wasn't really OK. And she had a bad feeling, a feeling that sooner or later her friend was going to wind up in big trouble.

***

'The Blackrock flanker is an animal!' said Tommy as he walked with Peter along the school corridor in Belvedere. 'You'd want to watch out; he broke the nose of the Clongowes scrum-half last week.'

Peter gave his friend a wry grin. 'You're really whetting my appetite for the match.'

'Just tipping you off.'

'Thanks.'

In spite of Tommy's warning, Peter was looking forward to this afternoon's rugby game. It would be a break from the continuing bad news in the civil war, where the army was gaining control of much of the country. It had reached the stage where Peter no longer enjoyed keeping his scrapbook of press cuttings, with the newspapers always biased against the rebels and the news so frequently bad. At times he even wondered if Annie might be right, and that maybe there came a point when you had to accept that you weren't going to get all you wanted.

He still hated the idea of giving up on a republic, though, and of swearing an oath of allegiance to the King, and his wavering views had hardened this week when the government announced that it was going to execute five captured rebels. Peter thought it was terrible that prisoners of war should face a firing squad, but that was going to happen on Friday unless there was a last minute reprieve.

Peter and Tommy reached the end of the corridor now, then encountered Mr McMahon.

'Off to play Blackrock, lads?' the teacher asked.

'Yes, sir,' answered the two friends.

'Don't take any nonsense from that crowd. Get stuck in.'

'Don't worry, sir, we will!' said Tommy with a grin.

As a fervent nationalist, Mr Mac was far more passionate about Gaelic games than rugby. Belvedere was a renowned rugby school, though, so he was obliged to take an interest in the school teams. The schoolteacher looked thoughtful and he turned to Tommy. 'Actually, would you do something for me before you go?'

'Sir?'

'Run up, would you, to Father Crosby's office, and ask him for the keys for the stationery cupboard.'

'Yes, sir,' answered Tommy.

'Good lad. You can drop them in to me at the staff room on your way out.'

Tommy left his kitbag with Peter, then headed off, leaving his friend alone with the teacher. Peter sensed that Mr Mac had deliberately got rid of Tommy, but the teacher very rarely discussed Peter's undercover missions in the school environment, and Peter was curious to know what was coming next.

'I wanted a quick word.'

'Sir?'

Mr Mac lowered his voice. 'Things are getting very hot, what with these threatened executions. So for the moment, I'm going to stand you down.'

'Stand me down? But—'

'Just a temporary measure. But the government is really getting ruthless.'

'Is that not all the more reason to fight back?'

'Don't worry, we will. But just till the time is right, I'm standing you down.'

'But I want to go on. I don't care if it's a bit riskier.'

'Your courage does you credit, but it's decided. It's no reflection on you, Peter. And no-one else need know. This is just between you and me.'

'But, sir– '

'But nothing,' said the teacher firmly. 'This is not a suggestion, it's an order. You don't try and contact me, or Finbar, or Ned. You keep your head down and wait for further orders. Understood?'

Peter *didn't* understand. *Why were they suddenly concerned now, when they had let him take risks in the past?* But Mr Mac wasn't someone with whom you argued.

'Understood, Peter?' he repeated, staring hard.

'Yes, sir. Understood.'

Mr Mac nodded, then softened his tone. 'Good man. I'll be in touch when the time is right. Good luck against Blackrock.' The teacher nodded again, then turned and walked away.

Peter stood in the corridor, awaiting Tommy, his mind racing. What the teacher had done didn't really make sense. Mr Mac wasn't the kind of person to do things on a whim, however, so there must have been *some* reason. But try as he might, Peter couldn't figure out what it might be.

PART THREE

PRIVATE WAR

CHAPTER NINETEEN

■ ■ ■ ■ ■

The kidnap took Annie completely by surprise. She had said goodbye to Susie when they finished school for the day, with Susie going to a piano lesson in town and Annie heading for home on her own.

She hadn't taken much notice of the motor van that was pulled in at the pavement, its rear door ajar, on the corner of Dorset Street. As she approached the van, a man emerged from the back.

'Annie, the very girl!' he said heartily.

He looked a little bit tough, but hearing him address her by name in a friendly tone made her stop.

'Your da asked me to give you a lift home,' said the man, and he put his hand on Annie's shoulder, guiding her towards the van door.

Briefly Annie allowed herself to be led, then she stiffened. *Something was wrong here.* The man kept a smile on his face but gripped Annie's arm tightly and firmly ushered her into the back of the van.

'No!' she cried, as he slammed the door shut behind them. She was about to scream for help, but the man clamped his left hand across her mouth, and with his other hand pressed a gun to her temple. He forced her down onto a large bale of hay that lay on the van floor.

'Don't scream, don't make a fuss – I promise you won't be hurt,' he said.

Just then, Annie heard the engine revving up, and she realised that he must have an accomplice driving the van. They pulled away, and the man spoke soothingly.

'I'll take away my hand and I'll take away the gun if you don't scream, OK?'

Annie's heart was thumping with fear, but she felt that she had no choice, and she nodded.

'Good girl. Put this on,' said the man, freeing her mouth and handing her a blindfold made from a woman's scarf.

Annie hesitated.

'Put it on! This time tomorrow you'll be back with your family – provided you don't know where you've been held.'

'Why are you doing this?' said Annie, fighting to hold back her tears despite the man's assurance that she would be free tomorrow.

'It's politics, Annie,' said the man. 'One day's captivity is you doing your bit for Ireland. Now put that on.'

Annie reluctantly put the heavy scarf around her eyes, and the man tied it firmly behind her head. She felt really scared, but she forced herself not to cry, and tried hard not to panic. There were lots of questions that she wanted to ask the man, but she knew that he wouldn't answer them. She would have to rely on her own wits, she told herself.

But why had these people abducted her? It didn't make sense. Normally, people were kidnapped for a ransom, but her family wasn't rich. And the man had said it was politics – so really there was only one thing that made sense. It had to be something to do with Da, and the dangerous work that he was doing, driving for the new government. But if they were going to use her to get at Da, what would they want him to do? And could she really believe that she would be freed tomorrow? A man who was willing to kidnap a twelve-year-old girl at gunpoint would hardly have qualms about lying.

She still felt really frightened, but she had to keep her head and look out for herself, try to think clearly. She attempted to figure out where they were taking her. It had been a crisp autumn day with clear skies and a promise of frost in the air, and when the van suddenly turned left, she sensed a flash of sunlight, the blindfold not blocking out all light.

The sun set in the west, so it looked like they were heading towards the north-western edge of the city. They drove on for about fifteen minutes, but with all the twisting and turning, Annie eventually lost her bearings.

'Here we are,' said the man when the van finally came to a halt. 'We'll be keeping you in the barn here, it's comfortable enough. Now listen to me, Annie, and be a sensible girl. We don't want to have to chain and gag you – so just give me your word that there'll be no screaming or shouting.'

Annie didn't answer at once, and the man continued.

'There's no point calling for help anyway, you wouldn't be heard. And we don't want to hurt you. So, just be sensible, right?'

'Right,' said Annie, figuring it was best to play along for now. She felt her arm being taken.

'OK then,' said the man. 'Out we get.'

★ ★ ★

Peter was embarrassed not to have recognised Mrs Reilly. He had met her the day that Annie's father had driven the four friends to Howth for the picnic, but that had been a short encounter, and seeing her now unexpectedly on his own doorstep, he hadn't known at once who she was.

The weather had been crisply cold all day, but the evening had turned frosty, and Peter tried to make up for his mistake by indicating the warm interior of the house. 'Please, won't you come in, Mrs Reilly?' he said.

'Thanks, son, but I won't,' she said, then she looked at him appealingly. 'She's not here with you by any chance?'

'Annie? No, I haven't seen her since yesterday.'

'Oh God,' said the woman plaintively. 'You were my last hope. She never came home from school today and I thought maybe … maybe she'd visited you.'

'No, sorry. Have you tried her other friends?'

'She isn't with Susie, and I spoke to all the girls on the Avenue. No-one's seen her.'

'And was she due home straight after school?' asked Peter.

'Yes. And Annie would always let me know if something changed.'

'Right.'

'I'm worried sick.'

'I'm sure it will be fine, Mrs Reilly. There must be some reason.'

'That's what I'm afraid of.'

'How do you mean?'

'I'm afraid she … she might have been kidnapped.'

Peter was taken aback. 'Who'd want to kidnap Annie?'

'I'm not supposed to say this. But her da often works driving government people. It's where he is tonight, and I'm … I'm afraid this might be something to do with that.'

Peter was stunned at the notion.

'I'd better go,' said Mrs Reilly.

'Can I … can I help in any way?' offered Peter, even as his head was reeling.

'No. Thanks all the same, son.'

'Are you sure? Do you want to use our telephone?' he asked, knowing that Annie's family – like most families in the city – didn't have their own telephone.

'No. You're very good, but I won't.'

'Are you going to the police?'

Mrs Reilly looked upset but she shook her head. 'No. I'll go and see my brother Mick first, he'll know what to do. Say a prayer, Peter, that she'll be all right.'

'I will, I promise.'

'Thanks.' Mrs Reilly nodded, then turned and set off into the night, hurrying away across the sparkling, frosty surface of the driveway.

Peter closed the hall door and straightened his shoulders, trying to steady himself. He was glad that it was a Friday night – his mother was in the drawing room with her bridge friends, and his father was working late, doing an emergency extraction. It gave Peter a breathing space to think uninterruptedly. And he had a lot of thinking to do.

Something was badly wrong here, he just knew it. And he had a horrible feeling that he could have been an unwitting part of it. Could Mr Mac have used him to get to Annie? The older man had certainly overheard them one night in the club, when Annie had been talking about her father doing risky work to earn extra money. Would Mr Mac kidnap a girl – a member of his own club – as a way to strike a blow? Peter felt sick in his stomach at the thought, but he couldn't shake it off. And it *would* make sense of something else. Maybe this was why he himself had been stood down so unexpectedly – to make sure he wouldn't be in the way. He felt a sudden surge of anger. Annie was his friend, and if Mr Mac was involved in this, then he had betrayed them utterly. And he wouldn't let him get away with it. He thought for a moment more, then made his mind up. To hell with being stood down, he decided. It was time to go into action.

CHAPTER TWENTY

▬ ▬ ▬ ▬

Desperately seeking comfort and warmth, Annie smelt the warm rubber of the hot water bottle that she had been given, and she sat back on the hay-covered floor of the barn, hugging it to her chest. It was a smell she strongly associated with home. On chilly winter nights, she loved to look out from her bedroom window over the narrow expanse of the gas-lit St Alphonsus Avenue, savouring the wintry conditions and the beckoning warmth of her bed, heated as it was by her pink hot water bottle.

The thought made her cry now, and she wished she was with her family. But after sobbing for a couple of moments, she steeled herself and dried her eyes, knowing that tears would get her nowhere. Her mother must be frantic with worry, and Da too if he had come home from work and heard she was missing. But there was nothing she could do about any of that, and thinking about it would only make her feel worse.

She had been locked in the barn for about three hours now, and had been treated fairly well. After being led through a house and into the barn, she had had the blindfold removed. Later on, they had supplied her with a large jug of water, a plate of stew, blankets and the hot water bottle. First, though, the man who had kidnapped her had forced her to write a note to Da, stating that she was all right, but confirming that she was held captive, and urging him to do as he was told. She hated going along with her captors, but the man had threatened her with the pistol. He had dictated exactly what she had to write, and Annie had been too afraid of him to refuse. He had left with the note then, and the food and water had been brought in by another man who sounded older. The second man had insisted that Annie stand with her face up against the far wall of the barn, and so she had never seen what he looked like.

Annie presumed that the older man had driven the van, and that perhaps the farm on which she was being held was where he lived. She had wondered at first how they had known her movements, but then she had reasoned that they must have found out where Da lived. Perhaps they had watched the house and discovered that she went to Eccles Street, allowing them to lie in wait for her. It was a horrible feeling to think that someone had been stalking her, and it suggested that these people were painstaking and smart, as well as being dangerous.

But she mustn't keep thinking like a victim or she would make herself even more helpless, she decided. And she was smart, too. So maybe she could use her brains to fight back. She began to consider all that had happened. She thought back on how long they had driven in the van, and she calculated that although the barn was somewhere rural, it couldn't be far into the countryside, and was probably just past the outer fringes of the city.

The location wasn't completely isolated either, because occasionally she could hear a vehicle driving past on a nearby road. And if she listened carefully, she could faintly hear what sounded like a river or stream flowing in the distance. As for the barn itself, it had a large rear door, and another door that seemed to connect it to the house from which the older man had brought the stew. Both doors were locked, and there were no windows, which made escaping difficult. But prisoners escaped from jails all the time. It was a matter of being daring and inventive. And with Da at risk, she had every reason to be both. She sat back on the hay, racking her brains, and trying to come up with a plan.

* * *

Peter dismounted quickly from his bicycle, crossed to the door of Willow Cottage and knocked firmly. He had no address for Mr Mac or Finbar, but the smoke rising from the cottage chimney confirmed that Ned was at home, so he would at least get to deal with him.

The door wasn't answered immediately, and Peter knocked again. This time, he heard someone approaching, then the door swung open. Ned looked shocked at seeing him, but before he could say a word, Peter walked past him into the front room, swinging the door closed behind him.

'What do you think you're doing?!'

'We have to talk,' answered Peter coldly.

'What the hell are you doing here?'

'I need some answers.'

'You shouldn't be here. You've been stood down.'

'That was between me and Mr Mac. How did you know?'

Ned looked a little flustered. 'I, eh … he mentioned it to me.'

Peter stared hard at him, and he sensed from the other man's unease that Ned had slipped up. Peter decided to go for broke while Ned was on the back foot. 'You're all in it together, aren't you?'

'I don't know what you're talking about!'

But Ned was a bit too quick with his denial, and Peter knew instinctively that the other man was lying.

'I'm talking about Annie Reilly,' said Peter.

'I don't know anyone of that name. But I know this. You were given an order. And soldiers obey orders – or else.'

'Or else what?'

'They face the consequences.'

'I'm not afraid of you,' said Peter angrily. 'And Annie is a friend. I won't abandon her.'

Ned looked at him appraisingly, then took a more reasonable approach. 'I'm sure Annie – whoever she is – will be just fine,' he said meaningfully. 'All right?'

Peter didn't answer, and the older man looked him in the eye.

'But if you want things to be fine for yourself, you need to follow orders. That means you turn around, walk out that door and go home. Do it now, Peter, if you know what's good for you.'

✳ ✳ ✳

Annie jiggled the tip of a hairclip in the door lock. It was a trick that she had read about in an adventure story. She hoped that she could copy the heroine, and escape by picking the lock in the door through which she had entered the barn. She had discovered that the bigger door at the rear of the barn was out of the question, being without a lock, but firmly closed on the outside – presumably with a bolt. That just left the door on which she was working, but the problem was that the book hadn't explained exactly *how* you picked a lock. She hoped that if she jiggled the hairclip around enough she might click back a lever in the same way that a key did. So far however, she had had no success.

She stopped jiggling and peered again through the keyhole. She could make out a darkened space with a line of light at its furthest end, and she presumed this was a passageway leading back to the farmhouse. Her interest now, however, wasn't in what she might see, but in what she had heard. It had sounded to Annie like raised voices, and she strained to hear further. Who was doing the arguing, she wondered? And what was the argument about? Could it be about the kidnap – and whether or not she should be freed tomorrow? Or maybe it was about Da and what might happen him? Before she had time to worry further, the voices grew louder. She couldn't make out exactly what was being said, yet one of the voices sounded strangely familiar.

Annie strained her ears, desperately wanting to identify the speaker. Then there was another, louder exchange, and she opened her eyes wide in disbelief. The older man who had brought her the stew had shouted, 'I told you to go home!' And a younger voice had answered, 'Not till you tell me what's happening!' There was no doubt about it. Annie was shocked to her core to recognise the younger voice as belonging to Peter.

* * *

'Will you cop yourself on?!' said Ned. 'This isn't some game. Lives are at stake!'

'Yeah, like Annie Reilly's. And don't bother saying you don't know her.' Peter was making a conscious effort to remain calmer than Ned. But the older man had hinted earlier that he knew about Annie, and Peter wasn't going to be fobbed off now.

'Do you know what day this is, Peter?'

'Friday.'

'Execution day. Five of our men, good men, went to their deaths today.'

'And that's all wrong,' said Peter. 'But it's not Annie's fault. And using her – that's all wrong too.'

'I'm not justifying myself to a pup like you!'

Peter moved closer to Ned and looked straight into his eyes. 'Is this where you're keeping her?' he asked.

Just for a fraction of a second he saw a look of discomfort in Ned's eyes, but it was revealing enough for Peter, and he sensed that his guess was right.

'There's no-one here,' said Ned. 'Now get to hell out of it before I give you a hiding.'

'I don't think so.'

'Fine, we'll do it the hard way,' said Ned.

Even though he was in his sixties, Ned was a heavily built man, and Peter knew he couldn't have overpowered him in a fight. He didn't retreat, however, and not wanting to let his nervousness show, he tapped into his anger instead and raised his voice. 'Yeah, let's do it the hard way!' Quickly reaching into the inside pocket of his coat, he pulled out a Webley revolver. He had retrieved it from the arms cache in the Botanics, and now he pointed the loaded weapon at the older man, his finger on the trigger.

'Take it easy, son!' cried Ned, instinctively taking a step back.

Peter made no reply, but felt a surge of satisfaction at the change in the man's attitude. He remembered the night he had escaped from the soldiers here, and he guessed where Annie was likely to be hidden. 'Give me the keys to the barn,' he said.

Ned stared at him, and from the look in the man's eyes Peter sensed that perhaps the older man was recovering from his initial shock at seeing the weapon. It would be important to get the keys quickly, while he still had the upper hand.

'The keys!' cried Peter.

But something had shifted, and Ned seemed more confident now. He didn't reply for a moment, then he spoke quite calmly, 'You're not going to use that, son.'

'Am I not?'

'No. So hand it over.' Then Ned held out his hand for the weapon and walked towards Peter.

* * *

Annie was rooted to the spot at the barn door. Her first emotion had been total confusion at hearing the voice of her friend so unexpectedly. Then her instinct had been to call for his help. But something had stopped her. *This was the lair of her kidnappers – yet Peter was here.* What did that mean? The idea that he might have betrayed her was staggering. She felt sick in her stomach at the thought. She strained her ears to hear at the door, but she couldn't make out what was being said now in the farmhouse, and instead her mind raced in circles. Could Peter really have set her up as a way of getting at some government official, via Da? Surely he wouldn't do such an awful thing. But the kidnappers were anti-Treaty rebels, and so was Peter. And today's executions by the government had probably infuriated them.

Even so, her mind rebelled at the thought of Peter agreeing to her kidnapping. She really liked him, and she knew that he liked her. She had also taken a big risk to save him on the night that she had lied to the police. Surely after all that he wouldn't put her at risk – and Da too, with whom he had got on really well the day they had gone on the picnic.

And yet, no-one but the kidnappers knew that she was here. And very few people knew that Da drove important government officials. Peter did, though. And Peter was here. Her heart told her that he wouldn't have betrayed her, but her head told her that someone had. And the evidence looked damning. She stood at the barn door, her feelings in turmoil as she waited for what would happen next.

* * *

Peter levelled the gun at Ned. His fingers felt shaky, but he steadied the heavy revolver by supporting it with both hands.

'Put it down, Peter, you know you won't shoot me.'

'Unless you make me. So don't make me!'

Ned gave a half smile. 'Not a bad line,' he said. 'But we both know you won't shoot me in cold blood.'

'It won't be cold blood if you force me. Now back off!'

'We're on the same side, Peter. Give me the gun and I'll forget this ever happened.'

Ned had been slowly advancing, and Peter took a step backwards, not wanting to allow him within sufficient range to lunge for the weapon. 'I warned you!' he said. 'Stay back. And throw me the keys of the barn.'

'I don't think so,' said Ned. 'And by the way, Peter, bad move with the Webley. Never take out a weapon you're afraid to use.'

'I'm not afraid,' said Peter, aware even as he said it that his palms were damp with sweat, but hoping that Ned wasn't as confident as he was making out to be.

'Yeah, you are, you're terrified,' says Ned, still slowly drawing nearer. 'And you're right to be scared. We know all about you. Where you live, everything. And we know how to deal with traitors.'

'You're the traitor!' Peter cried. 'You're the ones who betrayed me!'

'Hurt your feelings, did we? Maybe she's your sweetheart?'

'She's my friend. You shouldn't have touched her.'

Peter had been slowly retreating to keep his distance from the older man, but now he felt his back coming up against the dresser, and he could retreat no further.

'I'm losing patience, son,' said Ned. 'Give me the gun and maybe I won't give you the hiding you deserve.' He held out his hand confidently. 'Last chance, Peter. Give me the gun, right now.'

✴ ✴ ✴

Annie heard raised voices again, and her hopes rose a little. The first time she had made out Peter's voice the other man had been shouting at him to go home. Things had obviously calmed down since then but there had been a second flare-up during which she had heard Peter crying, 'You're the traitor!' Now the voices were getting angry again, and the more Annie thought about it, the more she felt that this was a good sign.

Supposing Peter hadn't been involved in her kidnapping? As her friend, he would be angry, then, if he found out, wouldn't he? And he might well argue with her captor. Annie wanted with all of her might for that to be true – for if Peter had betrayed her, that would be unbearable. But even if Peter was fighting her cause, it didn't mean that he would be able to persuade the other man to free her. Maybe he would argue only that she was to be treated well, and allowed to go free tomorrow, as promised. Or maybe he was arguing that Da shouldn't be put in undue danger – while still agreeing to their mission going ahead. Except that Annie somehow didn't feel it was that kind of argument. Something about it sounded more immediate, and she strained at the barn door to hear what was being said.

She made out Peter shouting, 'Back off!' and the other man shouting, 'Don't be stupid!' There was the noise of a scuffle and a chair being knocked over. Then Annie jumped back from the doorway, startled at the most awful sound she had ever heard. A single gunshot rang out, followed by an eerie silence. Annie sank to her knees, trembling, more scared than she had ever been in her life.

* * *

The smell of cordite hung in the air, and after the noise of the arguing and the loud bang of the shot, the room seemed unnaturally quiet. Peter stood unmoving, hardly able to believe that he had just shot a man. Ned lay sprawled against the kitchen wall. Bright red blood seeped through the leg of his trousers from the wound in his thigh. Initially Ned had looked to be in shock, but now his gaze cleared a little and he looked at Peter, his eyes blazing,

'You'll pay for this!' he said.

Peter was feeling a bit shocked himself, but he tried to keep his voice steady. 'Where's the barn key?' he demanded.

Ned ignored him, and instead pulled a scarf from his pocket. He wrapped the scarf around his thigh and began tightening it as a tourniquet to try to stop the bleeding.

Peter was relieved that he didn't seem to have done Ned life-threatening damage, but now he needed to find Annie.

'I said, where's the key?!'

'Go to hell!' snapped Ned.

Peter felt a stab of anger. Having come this far, he really had to find Annie and free her. He raised the Webley once more and pointed it at Ned. 'Don't make me use it again,' he said.

The older man kept the tourniquet tightly in place and looked at Peter, hatred on his face. He didn't answer, and Peter felt a little uncertain. Could he really shoot a man who was already lying against the wall, bleeding? Maybe not – but he had to act like he could. 'Give me the key or the next bullet is in your chest,' he said grimly. He aimed the gun at Ned's heart.

Still the older man stared at him angrily, and Peter wondered what he would do if Ned stubbornly refused to budge. He knew he couldn't shoot him in the heart. Even if he shot him in the other leg Ned might lose so much blood that he would be in danger of dying. No, Peter thought, he would have to bluff.

'OK,' he said, 'if you want to die, fine. You didn't believe I'd shoot the last time. Don't believe me now either.' He used both hands to take careful aim, then Ned's nerve broke.

'OK! Don't shoot!' Taking one of his bloodied hands off the tourniquet for a moment, Ned reached into his jacket pocket and took out a key ring.

'Throw it!' said Peter.

Ned steadied himself, then threw the keys.

Peter caught them, slipped the Webley into his pocket, and made for the doorway that led to the barn.

★ ★ ★

Annie shrank back in fear on hearing the key turning in the lock. She had sat unmoving since the gunshot, her mind going round in circles. What had happened? Who had fired the gun? Could Peter have been shot? Annie heard the lock clicking open, and her heart pounded even faster. She knew that she should turn and face the wall, but her worry over Peter put her beyond caring about the kidnappers' rules.

Suddenly the door swung open, and there he stood, his face flushed despite the cold of the November air.

'Peter!' she cried.

'Annie…'

'Thank God you're OK! I was … I was afraid you'd been shot.'

'I fired the gun.'

'Oh God,' said Annie.

'It's OK, he'll survive.'

'You didn't … you didn't help them kidnap me?'

'No!'

Annie looked at Peter, wanting to believe him, but still confused by his presence here.

'But you're with these people, aren't you? They're the rebels you've been helping.'

'Yes. But I swear, Annie, I'd no idea that they'd take you. I'd never have agreed to that – never!'

Annie could see that he was telling the truth, and it felt like a weight lifting from her.

'It was Mr Mac who did this,' said Peter.

'*Mr Mac?*'

'He's the one I've been working with. But he's stabbed me in the back. He's used us both.'

Annie was dumbfounded. She had always sensed that Mr McMahon was a strong nationalist, but she was horrified by Peter's revelation. 'I can't … I can't believe it.'

'He just used us. He doesn't care.'

'So how did you end up here?'

'It was a guess, after your mother called to the house looking for you.'

'God, poor Ma!'

'She thought you'd been kidnapped so people could threaten your father. And she said that not many people know about him driving for the government. But Mr Mac did – he overheard us talking one night.'

'Yeah?'

'And Mr Mac told me to stand down for no proper reason. It all fell into place in my head then. So I came to see if you were here, and if I could free you.'

Annie felt a surge of affection for Peter, and before she knew what she was doing, she hugged him.

'Oh Peter. You're a great friend!'

He hugged her in return, then drew back. 'We really should get out of here,' he said. 'Come on!'

Annie followed him down the dim passageway that led from the barn to the farmhouse. She was shocked to see a heavily built older man – presumably her unseen captor from earlier – whose leg was soaked in blood. His face was scrunched up in a grimace as he twisted the scarf that had served as Annie's blindfold around his leg, using it as a makeshift tourniquet.

'You'll pay for this, I swear it!' he shouted at Peter, spittle flying from his mouth. Despite the fact that Peter was hustling her out the door, Annie took a good look at the man's face, telling herself that she would give the police an accurate description of him.

Peter pulled open the front door of the cottage, and Annie followed him out.

'Where are we?' she asked.

'Cardiffs Bridge.'

'Cardiffs Bridge?' *Yes, that made sense!* thought Annie. She remembered the day of the picnic, and how Peter had knocked over their water, then gone to a cottage to get a refill. There had been something unconvincing about his clumsiness at the time, and now she saw that it was an excuse to visit this cottage. But this wasn't the time to go into that. She had to get home and raise the alarm.

As if reading her mind, Peter pulled his bicycle away from the wall and thrust it forward. 'Take this!' he said.

'What about you?'

'I've stuff to do here,' he said. 'You save your dad.'

'Will you be all right?'

'I'll be fine. Go, Annie, cycle as fast as you can.'

'Thanks, Peter.' She turned and looked at him. 'I'll never forget this,' she said, then she squeezed his arm in farewell, jumped up onto the bike and cycled at speed down the lane. Just as she turned onto Ballyboghill Road, she glanced back and caught a final glimpse of Peter standing outside the lighted door of the cottage. He raised his arm in farewell, then he was lost to sight and Annie rose in the saddle, cycling as fast as she could. The night air was cold and clear, and the bicycle lamp picked out the frost-laden trees along the side of the dark country road as she sped along.

The rush of cold air was bracing, and Annie tried to figure out what her best tactic might be. Should she stop somewhere along the way, perhaps, and try to ring the police? But there were few houses on the winding country road, and even when she got to Glasnevin, where there was more housing, most people still wouldn't have telephones in their homes. And then there would be the time it would take to explain that this was an emergency, and then trying to get put through to the right people in the police.

No, she thought, better to cycle home as quickly as she possibly could. She mapped out her route in her head – along Ballyboghill

Road, down the hill to the Finglas Road, then along the boundary wall of Glasnevin Cemetery, and finally down Lindsay Road towards home. Normally she would have avoided the spooky route past the cemetery, but tonight that didn't seem important. Instead she rose even higher in the saddle, pumped her legs furiously, and sped along the frosty road.

★ ★ ★

Peter stood at the cottage door, trying to get to grips with how he felt. He was still really angry that his former comrades had kidnapped Annie – it seemed such a wrong thing to do, even allowing for them being upset about the executions. As well as being angry, though, he was fearful. Supposing Ned bled to death from his wound? He didn't want that on his conscience. He thought about it for a moment, then stepped back into the cottage. Ned had risen, using a walking stick to support himself, and had fastened a makeshift bandage on his bloodied leg.

'Do you want me to call an ambulance?' said Peter.

'And have me arrested when they see a gunshot wound? You've done enough damage for one night, you little turncoat!'

'You're the ones that sold me out!'

'Keep telling yourself that, boy! But we'll get you. You'll pay for this.'

Despite trying to keep his face impassive, Peter found the other man's hatred chilling. How had he not recognised this extremism before in his dealings with Ned? And in Finbar and Mr Mac too? Had they always been fanatics, with him too blind to see it?

Had he been really naive in thinking that their fight for an Irish Republic had been honourable, when it now seemed that these were people who would stoop to any act to get what they wanted? It was awful to think that maybe he had been misguided all along. And frightening too, to know that these men might come after him for revenge.

It was time to get away from here. He held Ned's gaze for another moment, just to give the impression that he wasn't afraid of him, then he turned on his heel and walked out of the cottage.

★ ★ ★

Annie careened around the corner into St Josephine's Avenue, cycling faster then she ever had before.

'Watch where you're going!' cried Josie Gogarty who was walking back towards her house with a loaf of bread.

'It's urgent!' cried Annie as she mounted the footpath and made for the corner of St Alphonsus Avenue.

'Think you're great on your fancy bike!' cried Josie. 'Get that from one of your posh friends?'

Annie ignored her and cycled to her front door. She jumped off the bicycle, quickly took out her hall door key, and let herself in.

'Ma!' she called.

Her mother came running out to the hall.

'Annie?! Thank God!' she cried, wrapping her daughter into her arms. 'I was worried sick! Are you all right?'

'Yes, I'm fine.'

'Were you taken by–'

'I escaped, Ma,' interrupted Annie, 'but there isn't time for that now. Are you here on your own?'

'Yes, Da's gone out in the hackney, and Sean and Eamon are working.'

'I've got to reach Da!' said Annie. 'I have to let him know the kidnappers don't have me any more.'

'I've been trying to contact Mick,' said Ma. 'He'll know how to handle this.'

'There isn't time. We have to get to Da before anything happens. Where's Da working now?'

'At City Hall.'

'Where's the nearest big police station to here, Ma?'

'Eh … I suppose Mountjoy Station.'

'I have to warn them, and get to City Hall.'

'I'll come with you,' said Ma.

'No! Sorry, Ma, but every minute counts. I've a bike outside, I'll be quicker on that.'

Her mother looked like she was about to argue, but Annie was already making for the door. 'Just pray I'm in time!'

* * *

Peter's hand trembled as he opened the hall door and stepped into Botanic Lodge. He had heard of delayed shock, and now that he was safely home the enormity of what he had done was dawning on him.

He had found an old bicycle belonging to Ned in the yard of the cottage, and had taken it to cycle home, feeling that it would be wise to put as much distance as possible between himself and Willow Cottage.

He suspected that Ned would take the pony and trap and go to another safe house where he could have his wound treated. But just because Ned was likely to be out of action for a while didn't mean the danger had passed. Once Finbar and Mr Mac found out what had happened there could still be a high price to pay. He wasn't sorry that he had rescued Annie – he despised the way Mr Mac had used her – but he *had* definitely put himself in danger.

Peter crossed the hall quickly, not wanting to bump into his mother or any of her Friday night bridge cronies. He ascended the stairs, entered his bedroom and closed the door behind him. He needed time to think. What would happen if Finbar and Mr Mac came here seeking revenge? He still had the gun. But supposing his new-found enemies tried to burn the house down? It was a tactic that had been used a lot during the civil war. What would happen to his family then? Yet he could hardly go to the police and seek protection – if he did that it would emerge that he, too, had been involved with the rebels. He sat on the side of the bed, willing himself to find a solution as his thoughts went round in circles.

★★★

'Please, take me with you!' pleaded Annie. 'It makes sense!'

She was finally talking to two detectives in the nearby Mountjoy Police Station, but precious time had been lost. The desk sergeant hadn't taken her seriously at first, but eventually she had convinced him that she had been kidnapped and that her father drove important members of the new government. Now she was sitting in a room with two big, tough-looking detectives. They had questioned her closely on realising that there could be an assassination attempt afoot. Annie had answered all the questions honestly – with one exception. After he had risked everything to rescue her, she couldn't tell on Peter.

She knew that lying to the detectives could get her into trouble, but she simply had to protect him. And so she had invented a version of events in which she had escaped without Peter's involvement. The younger of the two detectives, a man with close-cropped blonde hair and small scar under his eye, spoke reassuringly. 'You've done really well, Annie,' he said. 'Leave it to us now.'

'But don't you see?' she persisted. 'Unless my Da knows I'm free, he'll still obey the kidnappers.'

'We'll tell him you're free,' said the detective.

'He mightn't believe you! He might think you're just saying that, because to you the most important thing is saving a minister.'

Annie could see that the older detective – a sallow-skinned, dark haired man with calculating eyes – was considering this, and she pressed her case. 'And that's if you can even get near Da without tipping off the rebels. But if I go with you, I can walk up to the hackney. Then he'll know he doesn't have to do what they say anymore. Please, it makes sense.'

'It's risky, Tadhg, for a young girl,' said the junior detective.

'So was escaping from the kidnappers!' said Annie. 'But my da's in danger and I want to help. Please,' she said, focusing on the dark-haired man. 'I'll be really careful, and I'll duck down the minute I've delivered your message.'

She thought that perhaps she had swayed the senior man, and she looked him directly in the eye. 'Take me with you! Every minute we waste here helps them!'

'All right,' said the man, suddenly making his mind up and rising. 'Two vehicles, Pearse, eight men, all armed!' he said to the junior detective. 'Let's go!'

Both men made for the door, and Annie rose at once and followed on their heels.

***

Peter dreaded confessing to his father. He had agonised in his bedroom for the last half an hour, but eventually had decided that there was no choice – he couldn't leave his family at risk. He walked slowly down the stairs, trying to rehearse how he might break the news. But there was no good way to tell your parents that you had been living a secret life that had gone spectacularly wrong.

In some ways it would be easier to break it to his mother, but she was playing bridge with her friends in the dining room, so he could hardly approach her. Besides, he knew that his father would be the one to decide on what action to take, so he figured that he might as well go straight to him now and get it over with.

When Peter had first come home, his father had been playing the piano, as he sometimes did to relax after a day in the dental surgery. He was a talented pianist, and Peter noted now that he had gone from classical pieces by Chopin and Schubert to more modern material – usually a sign that he was in good humour. At the moment he was playing 'After You've Gone', one of his favourite tunes. Peter paused at the drawing room door, trying to get up his nerve. He stood there a moment, then he knocked on the door and entered the room.

'Ah, Peter,' said his father with a smile. He continued to play the tune as he spoke, something that Peter couldn't do while he was playing.

'Dad, I've ... I've something to tell you.'

The smile slowly faded from his father's face, and Peter could see a look of concern. His father stopped playing and indicated for Peter to take one of the seats near the piano. 'What's wrong?' he asked.

'I'm ... I'm really sorry, Dad. You're going to be angry.'

'Spit it out, I'm sure it's not that bad.'

'It is, though,' said Peter. 'It's ... it's very bad.'

★ ★ ★

The police cars sped through the city streets. Annie sat in the back of the leading car with the two detectives, her nerves on edge. In other circumstances this would be a real adventure, but her fear of what could happen to Da meant that she couldn't enjoy the excitement of racing through the city. What she concentrated on instead was being inconspicuous – her fear was that the detectives might have second thoughts, and decide not to involve her in the rescue.

The unmarked police cars approached the quays at speed,

crossing the Liffey at Capel Street Bridge. Annie saw the sallow-skinned detective tapping the driver on the shoulder. 'Slow down now,' he said.

'Yes, sir.'

Annie presumed that the detective didn't want to alert the men who had blackmailed Da into obeying them, and she felt her pulses racing, knowing the key moment was fast approaching.

'Nearly there, Annie,' said the fair-haired detective, as though reading her thoughts.

'And when we arrive, Annie, you do exactly – *exactly* – what I tell you,' said his more senior partner. 'All right?'

'All right.'

'Good girl.'

The cars drove up Parliament Street, and Annie looked out the window towards City Hall, where several drivers were sitting in their parked vehicles, presumably awaiting government officials who were still inside the building.

Annie hadn't seen the Model T so far, and under her breath she said, 'Please, God! Please let Da be here!'

The dark-haired detective turned to face her. 'OK, Annie. Sure you want to do this?'

'Yes!'

'All right. Let's drive by City Hall.'

* * *

Peter told his father everything. He had half-planned to keep some of the details back, but once he began his admissions, it all came tumbling out. He felt guilty now for the huge problem that he had landed on his father, and foolish for having allowed himself to be used by Mr Mac and Finbar. He was still angry at how they had betrayed him and at the ruthless way they had used Annie as a pawn, and he felt frightened for his family over the threat that Ned had made. Most of all, however, he felt relieved. He had expected his father to get really angry – perhaps even to hit him – but while Dad had looked disbelieving and horrified several times during the story, for the most part he had stayed surprisingly calm.

'I'm so sorry, Dad,' said Peter now. 'If I'd known what I was bringing on the family … I … I'm just really sorry.'

'So you should be. You've been incredibly deceitful.'

Peter couldn't meet his father's gaze.

'You've also been remarkably foolish – wicked almost. Though I suppose in your warped thinking you felt you were doing the right thing.'

'I did, Dad,' said Peter, earnestly. 'I wouldn't have done it otherwise.'

'It was still stupid. And you lied outright to your mother and me. Having said all that, you're still my son. And no-one is going to harm you – or any member of this family.'

'So what are we going to do?'

'We'll have to send you away.'

'What?'

'We need to get you out of Dublin immediately. You can stay with Mum's relations in Sligo, and go to school there.'

Peter hadn't been expecting this and he must have looked shocked.

'It's the only way I'll be able to square things here,' said his father. 'I know some people with influence. If I play up the fact that you're a schoolboy who got in with the wrong crowd, and I move you for your own good, they'll probably accept that as the end of the matter.'

'Right…'

His father rose suddenly. 'OK, pack a bag quickly.'

'I'm going tonight?'

'We're all staying in a hotel tonight. It's not safe to stay here. I'll tell your mother and I'll ring John and Mary. I know they're both visiting friends.'

Despite being in shock at the idea of moving to Sligo, Peter was struck by the decisive way his father was dealing with things. Then a thought occurred to him. 'What happens, Dad, if they come tonight to pay me back – and there's no-one here?'

'They find an empty house. They'll never trace you to Sligo, believe me.'

'It's not that, Dad. If they find the house empty, they might … '

'What?'

'They might burn it to the ground.'

His father looked thoughtful, then shrugged philosophically. 'Then they burn it to the ground. I can't go to the police tonight. My approach depends on you already being moved to Sligo when I talk to them – and there'll be no more trains tonight.'

Peter looked at his father, taking in that he was prepared to lose the family home, if necessary, to make sure his son didn't end up in trouble. Peter felt incredibly moved, and wanted to say something meaningful, but instead he felt tears welling up and all he could get out was, 'Thanks, Dad.'

His father reached out and squeezed his arm briefly. 'Don't

worry about that now,' he said gently. Then he looked at his watch and spoke decisively again. 'OK, I want everyone ready to leave in fifteen minutes. You pack everything you'll need for school in Sligo. Go!'

Peter ran out the door and ascended the stairs, two steps at a time.

* * *

Annie's prayers had been answered. The Model T was parked around the corner from City Hall with several other vehicles. Annie had spotted it from Lord Edward Street when the police had driven at normal speed past City Hall in the direction of Christchurch. She had confirmed for the detectives that it was definitely her father's hackney. She had even briefly made out Da, sitting at the wheel and waiting for his passenger to emerge from City Hall.

Annie was hugely relieved, but she knew that the danger was far from over.

Meanwhile, the police cars had stopped about thirty yards up the street, and two of the policemen had gone back on foot and slipped into City Hall via a side door, to intercept the Minister on whom Da was waiting. Everyone else had got out of the cars for a final briefing by the leading detective. He said that the simplest outcome would be if the kidnappers were not in the vicinity, but had told Mr Reilly to drive a particular route, at some point along which they would intercept the car. In that case, Annie and her father could safely leave, and the police would launch a manhunt for the would-be kidnappers. It was more likely, though, that the kidnappers would want to control everything as it unfolded, in which case they were probably hiding out of view in the back of Mr Reilly's vehicle. This was a trickier problem, he said.

Annie's mouth had gone dry as she listened to him explaining their tactics – and her role in them. It had been one thing in the police station to insist that she wanted to help, but now that the time had come, she was scared. The policeman had instructed his men to try to avoid shooting because of the presence of Annie and her father. But supposing that all went wrong, and Da ended up getting shot? She could even be shot herself or taken prisoner again by men who had already proven themselves to be ruthless. But frightened or not, she couldn't leave Da in the hands of these people, and she steeled herself now as the detective finished his briefing.

'Ready, Annie?'

'Yes.'

'Good girl,' he said, then he handed her a bunch of red roses that he had bought from a hawker in Dame Street. 'Here're the flowers. We'll be strolling behind you, with two more of us on the far side of the street. Once you've warned your da, what do you do?'

'I hit the ground. And I stay there till you tell me it's safe to get up.'

'That's it. OK, Annie, good luck. You're a brave girl.'

The dark haired detective offered his hand, and Annie shook it. Her heart was pounding and she felt herself getting really scared. She wished none of this had ever happened. But it had happened, and she had to help Da, *now*, before she lost her nerve. She took a deep breath, partially covered her face by holding the flowers high, then started walking.

The briefing with the police had taken place out of sight of the Model T, but soon she turned the corner and saw it up ahead. There were two other cars parked along the side of the road, their bodywork covered in intricate white patterns from the hard frost that had come down. Annie was oblivious to the cold, however, and her pulses raced as she wondered if she was now being watched by the kidnappers. She felt really exposed as she walked across the frosty cobblestones towards the Model T, but she resisted the temptation to look around for the reassuring presence of the plain-clothes policemen.

It was only about five more yards now to the car, and Annie could see her father's face, his features gaunt as he stared ahead through the windscreen. He seemed so near and yet so far, and she fought back the urge to run to him, and instead kept to her normal walking pace.

Annie raised the flowers even higher so that the kidnappers – if they were watching – wouldn't recognise her before she got to the car. She knocked on the car window. 'Buy a rose, Mister,' she said.

Da turned in his seat, obviously a little startled by the knock.

'Only tuppence each, Mister,' said Annie.

Da looked at her in amazed recognition, and she quickly raised her finger to her lips, hoping he would get the message and not call out her name. He looked totally shocked, but obeyed her signal to be silent.

Annie quickly opened the door of the car, offering the flowers. 'Only tuppence for a rose, Mister,' she repeated. Once the driver's door was fully opened, she threw down the flowers. 'It's a rescue,

Da!' she shouted. 'Jump onto the ground! Jump out!'

Annie fell to the ground herself, as the policeman had told her to, but her father hesitated. From the corner of Annie's eye she saw two men rising from the back of the car, where they must have been hidden under some form of covering. 'Jump, Da!' she screamed, then there were shouts of 'Police! Drop your weapons!' Just as Da jumped, a shot rang out, followed by five or six more in quick succession. Everything seemed to happen in a blur then as policemen swiftly converged on the car.

'Drop your guns! Drop your guns!' screamed the police officers.

'All right!' shouted a voice, and Annie heard two guns falling. There was flurry of activity at the car as the policemen dragged the two kidnapers from the vehicle. A frightened Annie stayed on the ground as instructed, but she turned to see if her father was OK.

'Da?' she said. 'Da?'

He turned to face her, and Annie drew back in shock on seeing blood on his face. She remembered the first shot that had rung out, before the police had fired, and she looked fearfully at her father, terrified that despite all her efforts he might still have been wounded. Then he smiled, and reached out and took her hand.

'Am I glad to see you safe and sound!' he said.

'Your face, Da!'

With his other hand, her father gingerly touched his bloodied cheek. 'Must have cut it on the ground,' he answered.

Annie had never felt so relieved in her life. She grabbed Da's hand in both of hers, then she heard the policeman's voice.

'You can get up now, Annie,' he said, reaching down to help her to her feet. 'You too, Mr Reilly,' he added.

They both rose, and the policeman looked at her father's blood-ied face.

'Are you OK?'

'Yeah, only a graze,' answered Da, dabbing his cheek with a handkerchief.

The two kidnappers were brought forward, one walking, and one being carried by two of the policeman on a makeshift stretcher.

'Well?' said the senior officer.

'Flesh wounds in the calf and shoulder – he'll live,' answered the fair-haired policeman. 'If he doesn't face a firing squad.'

Annie looked at the two prisoners. The man on the stretcher was the one who had abducted her from school. Had that only been this afternoon? It seemed like so much had happened since then. The other man was Mr McMahon from her Irish language club, and she locked eyes with him angrily.

'How could you?' said Annie.

She had expected that Mr Mac might be ashamed, and perhaps would even apologise, but he looked at her defiantly.

'Five good men were executed today. That had to be answered.'

'By kidnapping a child?' said Da, and Annie could hear the con-trolled fury in his voice.

'We're fighting for Ireland,' answered Mr Mac. 'Everyone must make sacrifices. Even you and your precious child.'

Annie never saw Da move so fast in her life. Before anyone could stop him he swung a punch that knocked Mr Mac sprawl-ing backwards. The shocked schoolteacher fell to the ground and lay there, clutching his jaw.

'Nobody threatens my family!' said Da. 'If you ever look crooked at Annie again I'll swing for you!'

'OK,' said the senior police officer, 'take them away.'

The two policemen with the stretcher started towards the waiting cars, and two other officers roughly hauled a cowed-looking Mr Mac to his feet, then bundled him off after the stretcher.

The senior policeman turned back to Annie and her father. 'That's some girl you've got there,' he said, smiling approvingly.

'Isn't she just?' agreed Da.

'You were really brave, Annie,' said the policeman. 'I'm going to recommend you for a civilian medal.'

'Thanks ... thanks very much,' said Annie.

'And now you'd probably like a minute with your da. I'll see you both back at the car.'

The policeman turned away, and Annie looked at Da. His face was still bloodied but he looked at her with a smile that seemed a mile wide. 'I think I could do with a hug,' he said. 'How about you?'

Annie grinned and threw herself into his arms. He held her tight, and for the first time since her ordeal had begun that afternoon Annie felt completely safe.

Da gently stroked her hair and said, 'You're one in a million, Annie Reilly. You're one in a million.'

Annie smiled. Things had worked out as well as she could possibly have hoped. She was even going to get a medal from the police. But the main thing was that she had got Da back safely – and that was worth more than any medal. Her smile broadened, and she looked up at her father. 'You're one in a million too, Da,' she said, then she closed her eyes and hugged him even closer.

CHAPTER TWENTY-ONE

'Sligo? God, what will that be like?' asked Susie, sitting forward quizzically on the sofa in her family's drawing room.

'Don't know,' said Peter. 'I only visited, I've never lived there.'

'I mean, *Sligo* – it's miles away,' she complained.

Peter raised an eyebrow. 'That's the whole idea.'

'And where exactly will you go to school?' asked Tommy.

'I don't know. It was only decided last night.'

'I hope it's not some hedge school!'

'Thanks, Tommy,' said Peter sarcastically. 'But I think Sligo does better than hedge schools.'

The bright morning sun was melting last night's frost, and Peter looked out the window at the O'Neills' garden, the scene of so many adventures with Tommy and Susie. He wondered wistfully when he might see it again. Still, being here at all was an achievement. He had had to work on his father to let him come and say goodbye to his friends.

The family had spent the previous night in the safety of the Shelbourne Hotel, and Peter was taking the Sligo train later this morning. But however Sligo might turn out, Peter thought that it couldn't be worse than Dublin had been last night. He had had to tell his story again to his mother, to John and Mary, and had felt really guilty at seeing his mother in tears. John had become very angry with him until their father had told him to calm down, but Mary had been more sympathetic. Even so, it had been a nightmare having to confess all of what he had done.

Then there had been the worry that the house might have been burnt. Luckily that hadn't happened – he had seen from the distance that it was intact as his father had pulled into the O'Neills' driveway a few moments ago. Dad still wanted to get him out of Dublin urgently however, before contacting the authorities and re-occupying the house. Because of this Peter had just ten minutes to spend here before going to the railway station with the rest of the family.

So he had told his friends a much shortened version of his involvement with the rebels, and of the betrayal by Mr Mac – whom Susie had declared to be a 'double-dealing, stinking rat!' Peter had explained then about Annie's escape, and how she must have succeeded in getting to her father in time, as there had been nothing in the morning papers about any government officials being hijacked or shot. He told the twins how his father had refused to let him go to Annie's home to apologise, fearing that the Reillys might have him arrested, and how Dad had had to be persuaded to come here instead of going straight to the train station. And now his time was almost up.

'Sure, don't worry,' said Susie cheerfully, 'whatever the school, they'll have Christmas holidays. We'll see you then, won't we?'

'Yeah, probably,' answered Peter, although he wasn't sure if his father would think it safe to have him back in Dublin that soon.

'You'll be missed on the rugby team,' said Tommy.

'Thanks.'

'And I hate admitting it, but you'll even be missed outside of the rugby team!' said Susie.

'Thanks, Susie,' he answered, smiling despite himself. 'Will you give Annie a letter for me?'

'Of course.'

Peter reached into his inside pocket and took out an envelope with the Shelbourne Hotel crest on it, which he gave to Susie. 'Don't let my Dad see it; he doesn't want anyone else to know where I'm gone.'

'I'll deliver it in secret,' said Susie enthusiastically, then she slipped it behind one of the cushions on the sofa.

Just then there was a knock on the door. 'That'll be Dad,' said Peter, and they all rose. The door opened, and Peter saw his father standing there with Mr O'Neill. He wondered how much Dad had confided in his friend – probably most of the story, from the curious way Mr O'Neill was looking at him now.

'Time to go,' said his father.

Peter stepped out into the hall, followed by Tommy and Susie. Then Mr O'Neill came forward and offered his hand. 'Good luck, son,' he said. 'And keep your head well down for a while.'

'Thanks, Mr O'Neill, I will.'

'But even if you keep your head down, keep your sunny side up!' said Susie.

'I'll try,' answered Peter with a grin.

'Good luck, Peter,' said Tommy, and to Peter's surprise, there was a catch in his friend's voice.

All of a sudden Peter felt a little emotional himself, not know-ing when he would next see Tommy, who had been his pal for as long as he could remember. He didn't want to get all soppy, so he quickly held out his hand.

'See you, Tommy,' he said. 'Mind yourself.'

Tommy shook his hand, then Peter nodded in farewell and followed his father out the front door. They both got into the car, and Dad started up the engine. Mrs O'Neill was at morning Mass, but the other three members of the family came out onto the step as the car started up. Peter turned in his seat as his father pulled away along the gravel drive, and he saw Mr O'Neill, Tommy and Susie waving goodbye. He waved fondly in return, and felt a tear rolling slowly down his cheek, then the car rounded a curve in the drive and his friends slowly faded from sight.

★ ★ ★

Annie was having a strange day. After the dramatic events of last night, everyone had been pampering her. Even her brothers, Sean and Eamon, had been really nice to her this morning – and Annie figured that she might as well enjoy it while it lasted!

When she had finally come home with Da last night, her mother had fussed over them and made Annie drink sweetened tea, for shock. Annie had gone to bed, exhausted, and had slept through until ten o'clock this morning. The special treatment had continued then, and Da had brought her up breakfast in bed, including his speciality – fried bread made with rasher fat. Da claimed that using really hot rasher fat made the best fried bread in the world, and Annie loved the special occasions when he made it.

If all of that hadn't been enough, no sooner had Annie washed and dressed than Susie had arrived. She had made a big fuss of Annie, hugging her and telling her that she was a heroine. Susie had brought a box of sweets as a special present, and a letter that she kept hidden from Annie's parents, but which she handed to her later, when they were alone.

Quizzed about last night by Susie, Annie had sworn her to secrecy and told her how she had misled the police so that Peter didn't feature in the drama at the cottage. This had met with high approval from Susie, but she explained that Peter was still paying a price, and being sent away to school in Sligo. Annie had been shocked, but although she would miss him, she understood Mr Scanlon wanting to keep Peter out of trouble with the police, and out of sight of the anti-Treaty people.

Annie had been breathlessly questioned by Susie on all the details of yesterday's adventure, but eventually Susie pointed to the letter and rose dramatically. 'I know you're dying to read it,' she said, 'so I'll leave you to it.'

'No,' said Annie, even though she *was* dying to read it.

'I have to be back anyway,' answered Susie, 'we're going off to visit relations in Westmeath.'

'Oh, OK.'

'But I'll see you on Monday. In what land?' asked Susie with grin.

'In Ecland!' answered Annie, as her friend laughingly chanted it with her.

Susie had said goodbye to Ma and left. Now, finally, Annie had a chance to read Peter's letter.

She sat on her bed, eagerly opened the envelope, and began to read.

Dear Annie,

First of all, I'm so, so sorry for getting you into such a mess. I hope you're well after all that's happened, and that you and your father are fine. I think you must be, seeing as there was nothing about any kidnappings in this morning's papers, so that's good.

But I really wish you hadn't suffered because I was stupid enough to get involved with Mr Mac. I don't know what I was thinking, Annie. It seemed like an adventure, and that we were fighting for something good, but I shouldn't have got caught up with things I didn't know enough about.

Anyway, I'm sure Susie told you what's happening, and that I'm being sent to live in Sligo, and I have to catch the morning train. I'm really sorry I couldn't call to say goodbye, but Dad is afraid I'll be arrested, and wants to get me out of Dublin while he tries to fix things up with some people he knows.

I know that I'll miss yourself, Tommy and Susie when I'm in Sligo, but maybe Dad will let me come home for Christmas if he doesn't think that's too soon. If not, I'll see you sometime next year, either at Easter or at the very latest when the schools break up for summer.

Good luck in Eccles Street, Annie. I know you really love it, and no-one deserves to be there more than you. So go on and be Swot of – sorry – Student of the Year!

I have to go now, Dad is calling me.

With Best wishes till we meet again.
Your Friend,

Peter

Annie smiled as she finished the letter, but she also felt a little sad. Partly it was because Peter was being sent away, but also she sensed somehow that he wouldn't be home for Christmas, and that it might be a good while before she saw him again.

She hoped that she was wrong, and she hoped too that Peter would be happy in Sligo. And maybe next summer the war would be over and their little gang could all get together again and have fun like before. Was that just a dream? Maybe. But going to Eccles Street had been a dream too, and that had come true.

She remembered the way Peter had proposed a toast with his lemonade glass at one of their gatherings, and in her mind she raised an imaginary glass now. *Here's to you, Peter,* she thought to herself.

'Annie, lunch is ready!' called her mother from downstairs.

'All right, Ma,' she answered.

Anne smiled at her own foolishness, but finished her imaginary toast. *Here's to all of us staying friends.*

Then she re-sealed the letter, hid it safely in a novel on her bookshelf, and made for the door and her waiting family.

EPILOGUE

The civil war continued for several more months, but the army made steady progress in defeating the scattered rebel forces. In April 1923, the IRA Chief of Staff, Frank Aiken, ordered a ceasefire, and the conflict finally ended on 24 May when a further order was made to dump all arms.

Annie never saw Peter again. His family spent Christmas 1922 with their relations in Sligo, and the following spring Mr Scanlon bought a dental practice in Sligo town, and the family relocated to the West of Ireland. Mr Scanlon continued to play golf, and Mrs Scanlon became known as one of the best bridge players in county Sligo.

Peter stuck with his decision not to follow his father into dentistry, but did well in school and college and became a respected historian. In his late twenties he emigrated to Canada, and in time, became Professor of History at the University of Toronto.

Tommy studied to be a vet, and although he had to repeat his college examinations several times, eventually he qualified, and joined his father in the family practice.

Susie had no interest in college and went to work with her aunt, who was a buyer for one of the largest department stores in Dublin. She loved the work, and with a loan from her father she opened a clothes shop of her own. It did good business right from the start, although customers often asked about its unusual name – Ecland.

Mr McMahon was eventually released from prison, but he never got back his job as a teacher. He emigrated to Boston where he ran an Irish bar, and told stories about his exploits back in Ireland to anyone who would listen.

Finbar recovered from his wounds and escaped from custody in the final months of the civil war, but was shot dead while resisting the government forces in one of the last skirmishes of the conflict.

Ned also recovered from his gunshot wounds, and after a spell in prison for his part in Annie's kidnap, he returned to living alone in Willow Cottage.

Annie's father saved for and bought several more cars, and ran a small, but successful taxi company for many years. Although only in her fifties, Annie's mother died during an operation for appendicitis. She did, however, live to see Annie passing all her school and university exams with distinction and fulfilling her ambition to be a teacher.

Annie remained friends with Susie for the rest of her life. When Sister Josephine became principal in Eccles Street, she hired Annie to teach English and French, and Annie become one of the most popular and respected teachers in the school.

Over twenty years after she had last seen Peter, Annie came across a book that he had written about the civil war, which was published in Canada. Annie enjoyed reading it and was tempted to write to Peter, via his publisher, but in the end she didn't. They had different lives now, and the past was the past. And besides, there was no need to talk about the old days; she recalled them in vivid detail. And despite the dramatic way that tragedy had been only narrowly avoided, she would always have a special place in her heart for that time. No need to reminisce, she would always remember the action-packed six months when herself, Peter, Susie and Tommy had been the best of friends – and when she and Peter had the biggest adventure of their lives.

HISTORICAL NOTE

Taking Sides is a work of fiction and the Reilly, Scanlon and O'Neill families are figments of my imagination. However, the historical incidents are all real, and the major events that Peter and Annie experience, such as the burning of the Four Courts, the destruction of the upper part of Sackville Street (now O'Connell Street) and the funeral of Michael Collins all took place as described.

The Black and Tans that Peter encounters in the Prologue really were hated and feared by the civilian population. Regular British army soldiers were more respected, and some Dubliners even felt a little nostalgic when the last British troops marched down to Dublin's docks in December 1923, to leave forever the newly founded Irish Free State.

The Civil War lasted from June 1922 until May 1923. Approximately eight hundred soldiers from the national Army were killed, while the defeated anti-Treaty forces had between two and three thousand fatalities and approximately twelve thousand taken prisoner. Huge damage was done during the war, with railway lines destroyed, bridges blown up and houses burnt to the ground.

Because so many of those who fought in the Civil War had once been comrades during the War of Independence, there was a sense of betrayal on both sides, and the savagery of the fighting left a bitterness that continued for many years after the conflict ended.

St Alphonsus Avenue, where Annie lived, and Botanic Road, off which the Scanlons and O'Neills lived, are real places that still exist in Dublin. The fields leading down to the River Tolka at 'the steppiers,' however, are long since built upon, and are now the site of suburban homes in the Glasnevin/Drumcondra area.

Willow Cottage, where Annie was kept captive, is fictitious, but the location of the nearby Cardiffs Bridge is real, and there were cottages in that area. None of them now survives, and a new road and bridge occupy the site today, with the original Cardiffs Bridge, unused but still intact, the only reminder of how things once were.

Eccles Street convent, established in 1882, moved to a new location on Griffith Avenue in 1984. The site at which Annie and Susie attended school is now part of the Mater Hospital.

Belvedere College still stands at the same place in Denmark Street that it has occupied since 1832, and its rugby team, of which Peter was a keen member, continues to be a force in schoolboy rugby in Dublin.

And finally, the republic that Peter wanted so badly came into being twenty-seven years later, when in 1949 the Irish Free State became the Republic of Ireland.

Brian Gallagher,
Dublin, 2011.

If you liked *Taking Sides*, you will enjoy Brian Gallagher's other historical novel, *Across The Divide,* which follows the lives of two friends, Liam and Nora, whose friendship is put to the test when their families are on opposite sides in the dispute between the employers and the workers that led to the Dublin Lockout in 1913.

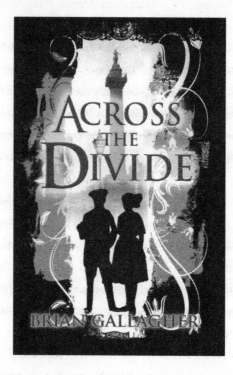

The book opens with a dramatic scene that captures the excitement, tension and atmosphere of the time. Here's a sneak preview:

31 AUGUST 1913
SACKVILLE STREET, DUBLIN.

Liam knew that he shouldn't be here. It was no place for a ten-year-old boy; any adult would tell you that. But he hadn't asked an adult. He had just sneaked into town without anyone knowing. Because really, he had to be here. Today's meeting in the city's main street was too exciting to miss, and he looked forward to telling his friend Nora all about his adventures later on.

Last night Liam had heard his mother saying that the police had banned Jim Larkin, the leader of the city's striking workers, from addressing the people of Dublin. But Larkin had insisted that he would appear in Sackville Street at half past one today, police or no police. Liam had no idea how Larkin was going to do it, and neither, it seemed, had anybody else, but the street was thronged with people eager to see what would happen.

Even though he was fairly tall for a ten-year-old, Liam found it hard to see across Sackville Street as he stood at the base of Nelson's Pillar, the high column topped by a statue of Lord Nelson that Ma said was the exact centre of Dublin. The thought of his mother made him feel guilty. She'd be worried if she knew that he was here alone and surrounded by grown-ups. And there was a funny mood in the crowd, a slightly frightening sense that something, anything could suddenly happen. But things that were frightening were sometimes exciting too, and Liam told himself that what his mother didn't know needn't worry her, and that if his hero, Mr Larkin, wasn't afraid, then he wouldn't be either.

There were hundreds of policemen on duty, and as Liam moved down the street towards the General Post Office he noticed how angry some of them seemed, fingering their batons and looking suspiciously at the people who spilled off the footpaths and onto the street.

The crowd itself was an odd mixture, with Larkin's supporters, mostly working men in their caps and Sunday-best jackets, mingling with well-dressed people coming from Mass in the nearby pro-Cathedral. Liam checked the time on the big clock mounted on the wall above a nearby shop. It was twenty-nine minutes past one. Only one minute to go, and still no sign of Jim Larkin. It would be really disappointing if he didn't show up, yet with policemen stationed at every corner it was hard to see how the leader of the striking workers could keep his promise. But he always kept his promises, Liam's father had said last night, you could count on it.

Thinking of his father, Liam glanced around nervously. As a loyal supporter of Larkin, Da was bound to be somewhere in the crowd. And Liam would be in serious trouble with him if he was spotted here. He would have loved to come into town today with him, but there was no question of his father bringing his son to a meeting banned by the police.

'Make way there, make way,' cried a big police sergeant, and Liam was jostled forward as a line of officers pushed the crowd back to allow a carriage to draw up outside the Imperial Hotel, directly across the road from the General Post Office.

Through a gap in the crowd Liam watched as a bearded, elderly man and an expensively dressed woman emerged from the carriage and made for the hotel entrance. Liam felt a surge of annoyance. Why should everyone else be pushed out of the way just because somebody rich wanted to enter the hotel? It wasn't that he had anything against the lady or the man – whom he now saw was stooped and slow-moving – but why did the police have to be so rough with everyone else? Da said that the police were completely on the side of the employers. So pushing the ordinary people back was a way of showing them who was boss.

Liam felt a tap on his shoulder.

'You shouldn't be here, sonny,' said a voice in a strong country accent.

Liam looked up to see a tall policeman looking down at him.

'Be on off home with you now,' said the man gruffly.

Part of Liam wanted to say 'Dublin is my home,' but it wouldn't be a good idea to give cheek to a policeman. He hesitated, reluctant to argue back, but not wanting to give in at once.

'Well, what are you waiting for?'

'Jim Larkin,' answered Liam, the smart answer slipping out before he could stop himself.

The policeman's face darkened. 'Don't give me lip, you little pup!' The man took a step nearer, and Liam drew back.

There was a sudden roar from the crowd.

'Larkin! It's Larkin!'

They began cheering wildly and pointing to a balcony on the first floor of the Imperial Hotel. To Liam's relief, the policeman turned away and began pushing his way towards the hotel.

Liam stood on tiptoe to see the figure on the balcony. It couldn't be! But it was: the elderly gentleman who had walked so shakily from the carriage was now standing erect and proud. It was Jim Larkin!

'Workers of Dublin, I said I'd be here, and here I am!'

The crowd went mad, and Liam found himself cheering loudly along with the people around him.

There was a sudden surge as police converged on the hotel, and Liam knew it wouldn't be long before Larkin was arrested. Sure enough, before Larkin could say much more he was pulled back off the balcony. But the briefness of the appearance didn't matter to Liam or to the people in the street. Their hero had outfoxed his enemies once again and coolly kept his promise to appear, right under their noses.

Liam ran forward, wanting to see Larkin in the flesh as he was led away. The people behind him surged forward too, but were stopped by the police, who had formed a cordon around the hotel. Standing as close to the line of policemen as he dared, his heart pounding, Liam saw a flurry of activity at the door of the Imperial. Then an officer in command of a group of uniformed policemen bundled Larkin out the door and towards a carriage.

Before Liam knew what he was doing, he called out, 'Well done, Mr Larkin!'

The tall union leader, still wearing the false beard that had been part of his disguise, turned his head towards the voice. Locking eyes briefly with Liam, he winked, and then was thrust into the carriage.

Winked at by Jim Larkin! Liam could hardly believe it. Wouldn't that be something to tell Da, if he dared!

As the carriage pulled away, scuffling broke out on the roadway near the hotel entrance. There was a cry of 'Baton charge!' and within seconds there was chaos. The policemen who had earlier been fingering their batons now suddenly wielded them savagely. People screamed in pain, and men fell to the ground, blood streaming from their heads and faces. Liam felt his stomach tighten in fear and he tried to run in the opposite direction, but was forced back by the crowd behind him who were being batoned by police officers advancing from the direction of Nelson's Pillar.

Turning on his heel, Liam ran as best he could down the middle of the road, dodging the bodies of those who had already fallen. He couldn't believe that the police were attacking everyone in sight. But something had been unleashed today, and nobody was safe, not even a boy like himself.

As if to prove it, a nearby policeman, having just felled a middle-aged man with a sickening blow from his baton, swung around and flailed at Liam. Dodging from an attack that might have split his head, Liam still caught part of the blow on his shoulder, and he cried out in pain.

Before the man could swing again, Liam ducked in panic under his outstretched arm and ran on down the street. Soon he was near the turn for Sackville Place, where he attended choir practice with Nora two nights a week. There was a laneway that ran off Sackville Place and parallel to Marlborough Street; if he could just make it to there, maybe he could escape from the horror of the riot.

He ran to the corner of Sackville Place and turned into it, then stopped dead. Mounted policemen were advancing towards him, reaching down from their saddles and felling anyone within range of their batons.

Liam turned and fled, the cries of those being pursued by the horsemen ringing in his ears. Sackville Street was now like a battlefield, but Liam didn't hesitate and ran diagonally across the broad thoroughfare, heading for Prince's Street and the alley at its far end that would take him to Middle Abbey Street and safety.

Lots of other people were running in the same direction, and he couldn't see clearly what lay ahead. Suddenly the crowd halted in disarray. Liam heard the order 'Reserves advance!', and the people in front of him milled about, trying to reverse direction as the reserve body of police officers was unleashed.

Really frightened now, Liam hesitated, not knowing what to do. People all around him began to be hit, trapped as they were in front and rear. Liam crouched and raised his arms to try to protect his head. A heavy hand spun him around, then a baton crashed into his temple. For a split second he saw a blinding light, then he fell to the ground and everything faded to darkness.